Péter Demény

The Magnificent Boar

Translated from Hungarian by
Jozefina Komporály

Originally published as *Vadkanragyogás*, 2017.

LIBRARY OF CONGRESS CATALOGING-IN-PUBLICATION DATA

The Magnificent Boar
Authored by Péter Demény

ISBN: 9798985965940
LCCN: 2022946349

ACKNOWLEDGMENTS

I'd like to offer my sincere thanks to the following:
Irén Arsene, who believed in my book from the start.
Jozefina Komporály who translated the novel into
English. Everyone who helped me along the way.

Is this what you call happiness? Smelling the stench of an old man? I screamed and flew out of the window. Basically, this was my only option to rule out finding myself coerced into something that was of no interest to me, just as I was once coerced into this life when I was born; it was my only, albeit phenomenal, chance, for which I was widely admired, to be honest, it must have been awesome, it must have been absolutely breathtaking as, blessed with the ability of flying, I just flew out of the window, being both human and half-bird, and then, aided by the breeze, I let down my magnificent hair, previously kept under strict control in the castle despite it always wanting to be left unruly, and also let myself go, unleashing my true self, because I had always considered this golden bird to be my real persona, my real self, the one that could find happiness, even though there was nothing to be happy about, and could experience freedom, despite life being nothing but drudgery with next to no flicker of happiness; so I just kept flying, soaring towards the sky, as if I wasn't the only bird but an entire flock, in the same way that I wasn't the only human being either, which is why I arrived at the conclusion that this had to be the reason why I could never be happy, and that this had perhaps led to another kind of happiness, out of the reach of those who didn't harbour a bird within them.

Meanwhile, an immense, heart-rending silence has settled in me, since a long time ago now.

My poor Diego! Ever since we hadn't seen each other, I stopped flying.

At first, I was just fluttering, whacking the air, even though I actually wanted to hit the sky, seeing that I couldn't reach God due to the impassable distance, that there aren't enough wingbeats that could take one to him, that said, I would have quite liked to perch on his window-sill every now and then, even if he didn't let me into his room; if I couldn't reach him, I should at least make it to the sky, I begged and shouted, only to myself of course, and I could have even been truly happy if, akin to the onetime king who had ordered the sea to be whipped, I could have done the same with the sky, mind you, the sea must have carried on billowing as if its surface hadn't seen as much as a single scratch; I kept flapping my wings like a fly in a jar, feeling constrained as I was, fighting for air inside a huge glass, no matter how large this inner space, one has a choking sensation, pressed down by what's not there, by what exists by virtue of its absence, and by way of its outlines through which one can perceive its boundaries; I kept fluttering and fluttering, rustling like a forest in a storm, by the end of which there were no trees left untouched, all my stuff got soggy, lightning harrowing my night, branches creaking and crackling, water trickling down the leaves in large drops, animals fleeing in despair; and then, peace and quiet being ushered in, the storm gradually calming down, perhaps I understood that there wasn't all that much I could have done, whoever is born into this world, has to live there, in this wretched see-through glass from which one can look outside but cannot know at what and especially why, why, why, considering that one is unable to fly out anyway.

It's equally strange, or in fact, not strange but rather typical of me—seeing that what was typical of me was called strange even by my parents—so it is strange that I was never afraid, though our fortress, this dark crow's nest, was situated at 2973 feet up on the Wunde, my father used to brag about this with a mix of pride and shame to pretty much anybody he could accost, as if pride and vulnerability weren't interconnected; so I wasn't afraid, this didn't even cross my mind, and in case anyone wanted to make me afraid, I would have stared back at them with consternation, what's the difference between 1000, 500 or 2000 feet, and besides, someone destined to fly shouldn't survive a crash anyway.

This restless, scared and rebellious flutter of wings was followed by a calm, slow flight; I must admit, it started out as resignation, I would have even cried if birds could cry, I would have flown like this for all eternity; but no, not like this, so the moment of peace and quiet had arrived, my heart was no longer pounding, it was only wanting to break, and then not even that, once and for all, I had left everything where I had taken flight from, it was no longer me but the bird I could have been and the one I was increasingly becoming, though this is also a case against me, I can tell that I'm going mad, I can hear the wingbeat of my ravens, but what is the meaning of this *against*, who said that humans were only human until

their judgement got clouded, could it be that this
very clouding is in fact the only true sharpness of
mind, I don't know, but I do know that by then,
in that moment I was so eagerly awaiting, I'd not
only be unafraid, I'd not only hear their wingbeats
but see their beaks wanting to gnaw at me, and
I wouldn't be able to write this something that
is only important to me, albeit more important
than anything, because I would no longer be in
the state of mind in which I used to be when I was
the person I am now, even though I'd much rather
be someone else and not me. It was precisely this
aspect of flying that I liked, namely that I could
so easily forget about living; everything changes
in an hour or two up there, in the vicinity of the
sky, in that inaccessible infinite, even time, let's
stick with that, I had swiftly forgotten about living
a human life, a confined pretence tailored to the
decisions of others, in which lies are known by the
name of love, and this is reinforced so stubbornly
that even those in the know fall victim to it; still,
in this case there hadn't been any talk of love, only
of this fine suitor who was to my parents' liking, so
obviously he'd be suitable to me, there he was, the
guarantor of my happiness, the prince of a small
faraway but sovereign and flourishing country, as

if I'd been craving after sovereign and flourishing countries and not someone whose touch I should feel even in the place I didn't know existed, or existed in me, in this ephemeral and changing body, in this human bird, so I could finally take flight not only spurred by disappointment but something entirely different, too.

This person was only twenty-four years older than me, my father explained, as if a single word could give me back the hope that had been taken away for good, he would have never used the word man, because then he would have had to acknowledge that I was forced to surrender my body to someone I had never met, someone who didn't even speak our language, and who'd penetrate me after all sorts of rituals as if he were my rightful owner, and I wouldn't even be able to reject him: a chattel shouldn't object but be happy about being appreciated. I kept muttering all sorts of terrible things to myself in the first phase of my flight, cursing my mother and father, who would have died much earlier had my wishes come true, I wouldn't have minded then if they perished, but now I know that they were both innocent and guilty for a reason and in equal measure: they confined me into this world, beyond the glass walls through which they couldn't see, so they had no idea about the existence of another world; those who can't see, don't even want to see; I was hoping, only after my initial flights, mind you, that they'd notice my ability to fly and thus would understand, be it only slowly and gradually, that their daughter was different from them, and if she was different, then this difference was real, that I had come from there twenty years ago, from this different world; but there wasn't much to hope for, when my beloved governess Mademoiselle Odile died, I flew out of the armoury, where I was taken at every important junction in my life, such as Odile's death and then mine, because there was no other way I could handle the situation where I learned of being destined to be the bride of Prince Nicolaus, they told me the news and I whizzed out of the window, disregarding everything, a reaction in which I finally showed signs of resembling my hapless parents.

I loved Odile because she was just as mad as me, she'd always carry a yellow fan, looking uninterested at the forest and, above all, at people, besides, the forest was silent, or to be precise, talked in an entirely different way than the world, the world my mother and father kept mentioning, what would people say, what did I care what other people had to say when my entire life, with the exception of a short period, was spent in accordance with principles I couldn't relate to, and neither could Odile, she kept stumbling about the forest, little bird!, she shouted cheerfully, placing a slight emphasis on the last syllable in her all-pervasive sweet French manner, which really suited her, fern!, she shouted another time, she always shouted, shrieked, cried with joy, I never understood what made her so happy, and perhaps this was why I myself couldn't experience happiness. God tends to punish those who expect something from him, one mustn't rely on him or expect anything from him, he must simply be understood, no this isn't it, one must accept what happens by virtue of him, and not seek happiness but rather find it in oneself, and Odile did find it, she knew how to be happy about anything, but this *knew* isn't the right word, there was no prior knowledge in this, nothing conscious, she was just hovering in the forest in her little blue hat, teetering among the trees as if she didn't know where she was, she'd vanish for half an hour or so, and I'd shake with fear, worrying about her, but then she'd emerge laughing and screaming, or rather she'd tumble out from somewhere, yellowhammer!, shouting with joy and rolling her R's with an aristocratic Frenchness, despite not giving a monkey's about aristocrats and their aristocracy; I'd never had better laughs with anyone about those two ridiculous creatures who were my father and mother, one time she charged out of the woods on the back of a wild boar, I had nearly frozen to death, wild boar!!!, tusks!!!, Odile whistled, and said something else, too, but I couldn't hear everything, I had never seen such a tame beast as that wild boar, it stamped out of the thickets like a tree-trunk about to collapse into an empty room, yet I could see on its face that it meant no harm, not to mention that it was positively fond of Odile, mind you, this couldn't really be any different because people who loved life as much as my Odile did simply had to be loved because they had a talent to impart hope impartially.

She perished in the plague, in that major epidemic of my youth, her magnificent girlish face was all suffering, her blissful body covered in lumps and bumps, she stank but still managed to stay beautiful and happy, radiating joy whilst in severe pain and sweating with fever, whenever the pain had generously let her catch her breath, she just kept shouting Katerina!, with her desperately rolled R's, that rising intonation, Katerina!, life is beautiful because death is on its way!, the last syllable of death was so high-pitched and so short that I ended up hating it forever, because I had now set eyes on it myself, having thus cheated on the very person I had loved the most at that time.

But don't we always cheat, in all circumstances, by promising things we cannot keep, affectionate love hasn't been tailored to fit human life and scale, romantic love even less so, you really mean it when you say this, yet you refuse to see that you are outside of the world, that for you *forever* is something entirely different, because you aren't in the dimension of time you are referring to, so what you are saying is both true and untrue, but the other isn't bothered by this ambiguity, either, because there is nothing less unequivocal in this world than affectionate love and romantic love, you give yourself to someone, entirely, without making lists, without weighing up pros and cons, without exercising caution, you just jump into the thick of it and don't want to come up to the surface, only that this very life will pull you back, it doesn't want to give up on its dues, clinging on to its rights, to its meticulously notched time, a time that will eventually be the killer of life itself.

I shall never forget the day of Odile's arrival, I knew that I'd get a governess, I was told about this more or less the way they let me know about my unfortunate husband, Katerina, we have to take care of your education, my father stated with a serious expression, as if they wanted to bury me, I had almost burst out laughing, they had already taken more than enough care, and who the heck gave a toss, I certainly didn't; prayers before meals, humble curtsies every time we saw each other, saying thank you after each course, and after the whole meal, a naturally more elaborate expression of gratitude, one had to say thanks for the roast chicken, as my mother put it, of course, she hadn't roasted any chicken herself, only spoke about the operation of cooking trout, frying pike, preparing common stinkhorns, soaking white bread rolls in chicken broth, does the god of chicken appreciate this, I once asked with an innocent expression, or the god of trout or pike, I added swiftly before they could have interrupted me; my mother nearly fainted, she clasped her hands in prayer, my father looked at me askance and replied, we'll find out when we invite them over, until then, it's enough if we thank the one true God we do know for everything; but I didn't know any gods, I insisted in vain, he didn't respond or appear to me, or I didn't see him when I should have, people say that the fact that I didn't meet him means that I was looking, and this further implies that he does exist, at times I had such thoughts myself and even held out hope, but now, as I'm putting these autobiographical notes to paper, I no longer delude myself with anything.

To sum up, my education consisted of prayers and polite bows, I don't know when they will set up the authority that forbids the education of children, or at least constrains it as much as possible, because if people like my parents dedicate their lives to education, you'll never learn about freedom; I was fortunate with myself and with Odile, and later with the person without whom I wouldn't have felt that I had ever lived, Odile arrived three days after my father's stern announcement, she was brought in a carriage to our fortress, my parents and I went to greet her, George, our servant of English descent, helped her, or rather wanted to help her step out of the vehicle, had Odile not jumped down and landed in her red shoes in our courtyard, her yellow bundle hovering in the wind, she then looked up at the seven turrets my parents were so immensely proud of and burst out in roaring laughter, my mother and father looked at each other with indignation, they will no doubt pray an awful lot in penitence, I mused cheekily; *centaur*, Odile said when she finally managed to catch her breath, now I know that she didn't actually say this, but that's what I heard, with a long and strange U sound, followed by an equally weird R, soft and flirty, to stay with you forever, and then I instantly knew that one could only love Odile, I shall love Odile, and feasted my eyes on my parents with a look of love that made them hold on to each other in bewildered fear.

I scolded them, in a way that many people would probably find blasphemous and reprehensible, rolling their eyes, but back then, when I was forced to break up with my beloved Diego, or he left me, or life made us leave each other, oh, love, why are you so complicated, even when it comes to sheer grammar, so I flew home, a short flight in those distant mountains wouldn't have sufficed, this pain wasn't just larger than myself but larger than life, larger than everything I had experienced and will experience, larger than what I could ever live through, this pain is what I want to address in these memoirs, it is the very reason for writing in the first place, but I'm still too weak for this, my body is ready but my soul is feeble; after Odile's death I couldn't do anything apart from keeping a diary, flying wouldn't have been able to channel all the tension comprised in my life, being the mad one among the drab, deprived of the only fellow mad person, with whom we spoke the same language, had the same thoughts, and if not, then just ended up laughing at the same things, besides, I couldn't always fly anyway, since flying didn't just depend on me but also on the pain that would literally give me wings and lift me up among the birds of the sky; the latter was, however, entirely or almost entirely unpredictable, which is why at the age of sixteen, on the day after Odile's death, I started writing my diary and this turned out to be the best decision of my life; so that people who lay hands on these confessions shouldn't turn into a pillar of salt, Diego wasn't my decision but my destiny, he crossed my path owing to life itself, I hadn't chosen him as I hadn't chosen flying, which was a gift from the sky, the diary, however, was my initiative, it was me who realised that there was no other way out, this was my only chance of not going insane, or what's worse, not ending up like my parents, these two well-bred crows, whose wings were only there to cling to their bodies; behold this terrifying blank sheet of white paper on which I have to write, I said to myself when I first took a seat at my desk, more than an hour passed, and after that, the pages kept filling up as if I'd never done anything else in my entire life, and every time I took a break, I'd think that there was so much going on within, people had no idea what was pulsating in their soul, I also remember wondering as I was writing my diary about the inner self, and musing about the consistency of the human soul.

I received no answer to this latter question, or to be precise, I didn't find an answer, most probably it would be like a hugely swollen cow's udder that barely needed touching before spurting milk, so one could barely produce enough pails to scoop it up, in any case there was no doubt that all this was a matter of temperament, on the one hand, and state of mind, on the other, my soul had always resembled cow's udders despite my prayers for it to not contain anything, so I could calm down a little at long last, and not crave after flying or writing, just sit there like an oriental sage, just live, come and go, eat and drink or make love, but instead I kept sulking, nearly bursting at the seams, out of sorrow rather than joy, and I should add that not even God, if he existed, could deny this, but this time it was up to me to admit that happiness, when it had finally arrived, transformed my soul so profoundly that it could have easily engulfed twice the amount; mind you, I had never found it wanting, I could have simply carried slightly more.

I wouldn't have been able to endure this sensation of fullness had I not started this diary, this was the reason why I filled so many pages with my notes and looked after them as if they were the apple of my eye, my parents knew that I was keeping a diary but could never actually find it, I'm convinced that they had tried to lay hands on it, they looked everywhere but they failed to track it down, I had hidden my life really well, besides, they wouldn't have understood what I had hidden and what they discovered in case they found it; when I flew home after Diego's departure, however, soaking with rain and landing with drenched wings on the windowsill, I knocked on the glass pane with my tired beak and after some time, my mother's silhouette emerged in the dusk-filled room, first she quickly covered her mouth with her hand, then let me in, still trembling, as soon as I had regained my human shape and caught my breath, I was about to tell them what had happened, at that stage I wouldn't have been able to grab a pen and the flight wasn't quite enough, either, I needed someone to listen to me, an actual human being who loved me in his or her own way even if he or she couldn't understand me, or at least (oh, I contended myself with so little then!) had something to do with me; at that point my mother signalled that I should stay silent, she asked me to dance and started to throw the kind of shapes I had learned from my Diego, the ones we threw so happily on the day we first met, at our initial encounter that marked the start of our love, or, as I now know, its arrival; it's always hard to keep love apart from its manifestations, in the endless moments of torturous absence it isn't easy to persuade the heart that love *does exist*, it's not just some fantasy, you can of course swear to this as far as your own commitment is concerned, but when it comes to that of others, this only applies if they join you where you bury your face in the pillow, and then that's all you can do, I for one have always done that, until I fell asleep in the middle of this sweet remembrance of wonderful memories and these episodes springing from times past that reassure you that there is indeed something that binds you to that man, and even though by now everything has turned into a lie, seeing that he isn't here, he doesn't miss you, *back then* none of this could have been a lie, you could see this in his eyes, and later feel it in his embrace, his extraordinary hard-on was just as incapable of lying as your, for him equally delightful, slippery wetness, that was longing precisely for this thrusting hardness and could never get enough of it; my mother bowed, moving backwards and then forwards, just like my Diego who I knew would never ever dance again, but I was unable to grasp how my mother could possibly be aware of what had happened between us, I had never written any letters, and though she could have heard this-or-that from the odd ambassador, their only concern was politics, they couldn't care less about me, yet my mother knew, I was able to tell from her large gestures and impeccable sense of rhythm that she could understand and relate to everything, she really understood me, it was at this point that I realised that I had misjudged my parents too soon and too easily, even in the seemingly drabbest soul there is a spark that has nothing to do with formalities, perhaps this is mankind's love, mankind's knowledge and instinct accumulated over thousands of years, I have no idea, my mother kept fluttering and dancing with great ease, and I had no idea about this, either, she kept bowing while leading me gently but firmly, and in the end, I heard my father, whom I hadn't noticed until then, Katerina, have some dinner, you must be tired, from these few words I could gather that he was also in the know, after all they must have once been in love, too, albeit not with each other, and what's more important and what comforted me that evening was that they had actually loved me after all.

No, flying didn't really depend on me but on Odile, she started it, after we had a good laugh about our fortress with the seven turrets and she settled in her room, shoving her stuff down, I can imagine what this looked like, in case my parents expected my governess to teach me about law and order, they couldn't have made a bigger mistake, in any event, she couldn't have taught me about something they would have called order and taken seriously, specks of dust were not meant

to settle on our furniture, my parents had lead a
fierce life-long battle with dust, our fortress had
always looked as if it had been freshly polished
with the most exquisite range of cleaning prod-
ucts and thereby ended up practically deprived
of life, even my father's beloved hunting dogs
weren't allowed to ramble at leisure, seeing that
they were losing their hair, everything and everybody was dangerous in some way, as if the great
architect of our lives had allocated us our respec-
tive spaces with a giant compass, dear mother,
dear father, what were you so afraid of, see how
much compassion was needed for this simple
question, and how much love to arrive at compassion, and how much Odile, Odile, Odile, Odile
to arrive at love, Odile who had come over to my
room as soon as she had dropped off her belong-
ings, she came over and started to sing, *alouette,
gentille alouette, alouette, je te plumerai*, she sang,
while producing a piece of paper, no, the paper
just appeared somehow in her hand together with
a pen, she drew a skylark, this was also amazing
about her, but what wasn't?, back then I couldn't
yet speak French, so I couldn't have asked what
she was drawing, but later, when I could, I still
didn't have to, whatever she drew was obvious

to me, it wasn't just any old bird but a *skylark*, and there was no hint of doubt about this whatsoever, I kept staring at this skylark, and wasn't envious of its beautiful singing voice but its wings, while Odile, and this was the other amazing thing about her, didn't appear to pay attention to anything except herself and her own goofiness, yet she always observed everything and never needed any clues, one didn't even notice the passage of time and she arrived at a conclusion at the same time as the experience of emotion, or in the case it wasn't an emotion but some unknown truth, she still couldn't refrain from stepping into the realm of this truth, and from that moment onwards, she actually knew, and even asked, *voulez-vous voler?*, the very instant when, trembling with desire, it had occurred to me how nice it would be to take flight, how wonderful it would be not to care about anything and anybody, just fly out of the window, flapping my wings and soaring away, free from desire or memories, Odile opened the window and waved, *allez*, and when I stared back at her in bewilderment, how could I possibly fly, I have nothing to fly with, she literally scolded me, *allez, allez*, signalling to whisk off, and I had suddenly sensed an unexpected strength in me and took to the air, and that's when I understood that if you set your heart on something you shouldn't just wait but really-really vie for it and then you'll be granted all your wishes.

II

It's equally uncanny that when you want something, you already know full well that you want that very thing and nothing else, you have no doubt whatsoever regarding what you want; this is the way selfishness comes about, after all, this is just another word, a sombre one at that, much like a disgruntled confessor; those who are selfish only think of themselves at all times and without fail; what a simple definition, like any other definition offered up by the police chief, my father quite enjoyed having the odd glass of wine in the company of his confessor, a tall and sluggish chap, sweating even in the deadliest of winters and water streaming down on him so that his Bible, which he always carried with him and held in his hand, was practically soaking wet; he made a habit of citing Biblical passages at the most unexpected times, and when he was doing this, he simply came to a halt, be it on the stairs, the corridor, under the arches, absolutely

anywhere, his favourite was *The Book of Proverbs*,
'My son, if sinners entice you, do not consent', he
cited, he had a slight lisp but otherwise had perfect diction, one could sense that he was proud of
this achievement and was getting above himself,
he must have thought that good pronunciation
was a cornerstone of faith, or at least its cross-
beam, poor pious fool, 'my son, do not walk in
the way with them; hold back your foot from their
paths', he used to say with a cloudy gaze, utter-
ing the words so slowly as if he wanted to weave
them around the whole wide world; once I almost
crashed into him as we were heading to the chapel
not to miss morning prayers, every so often it was
this moron's turn to lead the prayers, this joke of
a man acting as a steward of faith, and as we left
the dining room making our way down, he must
have sensed my inner reluctance and wanted to
teach me a lesson, making it clear once and for all
that whatever was to happen was the right thing,
and it was exactly right in this way; my parents
were walking in front, followed by Father Roge-
rius, whom we used to call Father Brouillard with
Odile, though my own father, who had once
caught us in the act, suggested that we should
have called him Father Nuit, Odile was right

behind me—and one could tell that my parents wouldn't have dared to tell her off for anything in the world, her initial introduction ended up rather unique and therefore entitled her to some liberties—this time, Odile was accompanying me not so much out of duty but because she was thus able to laugh most heartily at this professed idiot; Father Brouillard must have felt the fiery breath of my doubt on his back and came to such a sudden halt that I almost fell over him, I could barely hold back from somersaulting down the stairs, Odile broke out giggling, but this couldn't touch his holiness in the least, 'discretion will watch over you, understanding will guard you', he recited with his index finger held up, at which point I noticed that this finger was much longer than his middle finger, at least by half a span, it was heading skywards with reckless stupidity, so I had to cackle, too; meanwhile, Father just let his words echo, standing there in the thick silence for at least a minute, as my parents were watching all this agape, in the end he graciously let his God-grown finger down, turned around, and we were finally able to move along, well, he would defi-nitely watch over you, Odile whispered in my ear and we burst out laughing again, one simply can't face up to this much Christianity with a serious face; Father Brouillard would most probably have a few candid words or passages about selfishness to say, but as usual, he'd be wrong, love is actually rather selfish, can't even be any different, seeing that when something unexpected has finally become part of your life, you can't just let it go, for this, one would not only have to be a saint but considerably more, and above all, more inhuman. He had something to say to everyone, one time he was preaching about bringing up girls, as I now suspect at my parents' request, but back then, we were just listening to him with Odile and didn't understand a word, I mean we did understand the actual words but not *their overall point*, the intention behind his preaching, does this man still think that he can knock me into shape?!, this was hard to believe, so we kept thinking about this during his entire oration, except when we couldn't refrain from giggling, a behaviour immediately noted with a frown by my father, by the end, he didn't even have to turn around, we could already imagine this from behind his back, we could sense that it was time yet again for a frown and continued to giggle, all this was particularly edifying first thing in the morning, 'it is not enough for Christian parents to just take care of their sons and daughters when they are ill, to seek out doctors or mourn their children's death, they also have to understand that the children they give life to are born into this world for God, and parents will be severely punished if they don't raise them according to God's will,' Father Brouillard broke into his preaching in the chapel, which shook up our joy at once; today, I wouldn't be so cheerful, at times, I even have the heretical thought that it would have been better and God would have helped me much more if I'd been like my parents and everyone else, I would have been less happy but would have certainly suffered less, it's also worth taking into account how closely connected these aspects are, who is less happy is also suffering less, mind you, this isn't entirely true, some people have more than their fair share of suffering in this earthly misery; I for one was unable to lead an ordinary life, I simply wasn't cut out for it and was deeply troubled by the fact that there was such a thing in the first place; I remember once I started crying over lunch, a fabulous lunch for which any other child would have been most grateful, servants everywhere, carrying huge platters of the finest dishes, Jacob, the head chef, bowing and nodding in front of my father, who was tasting the various courses with a frown, and in the end, by the time the head chef was entirely covered in sweat, he finally indicated with a slight wave of his hand that they could serve what they had prepared, I don't recall what he settled on in the end, quail pâté perhaps; no sooner had Jacob felt a sigh of relief than I started screaming, so bitterly that everyone ended up scared stiff, I was about five years old, everybody jumped up or, in case they were already standing, started running up and down, this presumably made me even more anguished, I stopped eating for days, weeks, even months, yet I continued to retain in my mouth the unforgettable taste of nothing, or perhaps not of nothing but of *the habitual*, of something endlessly repeated and unchanged, and as I kept growing, I continued to hope that I wouldn't live like this, that one day there'd come a time when I really wouldn't, only to fall back yet again into this endless cycle of boredom and block everything and everyone that could poten-tially lead me away from here, because there is no other form of loyalty than bitter remembrance.

My day-to-day existence was good for three things: firstly, to live, or rather to survive; secondly, to be tossed around like a vessel on the sea and meanwhile watch from the corner of my eye what was happening around me, and years later find myself marvel at familiar objects, occurrences or gestures despite not knowing where I'd encountered them before, I had often come across such situations, being a foreigner in my own life; and thirdly, to despise it, so that I'd never ever want to live by it or in it, but instead seek delight in anything sizzling, rattling, swishing and knocking on life's ledge like a gust of rain, and only consider suchlike as true and joyful; and then to immerse myself into it again, and find, both in fear and in resignation, that I too was able to live like this, like my parents, with the same impassivity and wisdom, and although I have always had an inkling about the former, and even admitted this to myself, I actually needed an awful lot of disappointment, including the ultimate blow, for the latter.

I can't recall the entire sermon by heart, I've burnt all my diaries in which I could most probably find this information, however, I can still recall the juicy allegories of this moron, that's when I first realised that passion can channel wisdom even into the most stupid person and give them wings, 'I have seen a roe being breastfed by a hound, and behaving just like an actual canine', he said and I looked at Odile, who was about to burst out laughing, 'which is why, from a drunkard, lewd and wrathful nurse, an innocent child imbibes a predisposition for similar morals. For this reason, Saint Jerome recommends that mothers should breastfeed their children themselves if their strength and health allows', while I kept thinking that if this were quite so simple, why wasn't I more like my mother, why was I completely different, after all, she was the one breastfeeding me, I was entirely certain about this, seeing that it was my rarely emotional mother who revealed that as soon as she had realised that whatever she had to say was in vain, her eyes blurred, her face turned carmine red and she raised her arms towards the sky and shouted, what could I have possibly done wrong to see my only daughter betray me? She was *beautiful*, even more so because she transcended her insignificance in vain, and shouted, why her, whom I had suckled on my own breasts?!, and I could see that she was trying to grab her chest, pulling on her garments, but they'd naturally not yield, oh, why can't I rip them off!!!, she shouted like an amazon and then turned around and left me, all dismayed. This outburst left me astounded at my mother's ability to behave differently from her usual ways, this was a clear indication of how little I knew about life, but what could I have possibly known?!, and what could I have learnt by listening to my parents and this Father, although I should definitely thank him for drawing my attention to love songs, from which he wanted to keep me away, but his interdiction only had the opposite effect and I would have done anything in my power to have access to them, but our library couldn't pride itself on too many books anyway and such volumes were carefully removed from its collection, if I remember correctly, Father was the one to organise their withdrawal, besides, I was only allowed to read in the library under his supervision; on a summer night, however, when I thought I'd never be able to read any love songs until I had left my family home, a piece of parchment knocked on my window and when I carefully sneaked a little closer, I was handed a note which read, *Fhlower you should know that I must leave you, and fhor your sake, I'll have to clothe myself in mourning,* I don't know what had happened to me but I could barely stagger back to my bed, after which I burst out crying, buried my head into my pillow and just kept sobbing, I was hoping that Odile would come to see me, but she must have been in a deep sleep and only the stars were shining bright and indifferent until, once more, I managed to cry myself to sleep. Now I know why I had to cry, though I still don't understand why God has to warn people in such an ambivalent fashion: so you can tell that you've been warned except that you are unsure about what, in your life at that time there is nothing to give you an idea about what it will be like when you eventually understand, you might have some inkling, but this inkling isn't worth mentioning; mind you, this might be the best part, given that if we anticipated what was about to happen, we wouldn't be able to experience anything properly, I was fighting with hypocrisy and reason all my life, this is why I ended up alone, although I have always valued intelligence and honesty, credibility or however I should refer to the opposite of hypocrisy, the notion that someone doesn't just say something or behave in a certain way for the sake of appearances, tradition and other restrictions, but because they simply believe in it, and most importantly feel it, they proclaim it from within and not just mimic this *inner* expression,

I can see in their face, eyes and entire being that they really think so, this is the most wonderful thing about love, that despite being engulfed in doubt—the latter because unexpected fortune triggers exquisite pain—asking yourself how long it will last, why did they fall in love with you, do you deserve this, and if so, will they let you deserve who loves you, those in love are seemingly running after a carriage that is charging ahead, and they can keep up for a while, doing their utmost not to be left behind, but the horses are galloping, hooves are trampling, the whole world is pounding like a bitter heart, and in the end, despite all the effort, they end up being left behind, *a racing cart*, this is what it is, not a carriage, that's too exclusive and elegant, when in fact love is somewhat ordinary, amazing that it can also be, it doesn't cover its mouth when using a toothpick, at times, you can see absolutely everything, but you don't mind, you have never seen me like this, which is also down to love by the way, and by extension to the person who had brought love into your life, although the latter is in fact rather innocent, he was minding his business, getting up in the morning and going to bed at night, washing, having breakfast and making his way wherever it was necessary, or wherever life was taking him, life can really take people all over the place, at times, you may think that nothing will ever happen, you don't even have a heart anymore, only some organ that makes you believe that you are alive; Odile had views on this matter, too, *l'amour*, she said with a sigh, as if she was dismissing it with a wave of her hand, *l'amour* is like a skylark, when she said this, she had already learnt a few words in my mother tongue, flying in, flying out, regardless of the *fenêtre*, she added in her delicate Frenchness, and soon I had experienced myself how irrelevant it was indeed, love charges in and you may well run to the window, it still shows you that you are in fact covered in wounds, as it happens, nothing makes you happier than your wounds, you don't even try to protect yourself anymore, when it hurts you finally feel that you're well and truly alive and find it hard to come to terms with what you had hitherto called by the name of life.

III

You understood everything, Odile!, I tend to cry out every now and then, either to myself or not just myself, it has been twenty-one years since the skylark flew out of my life for good, I was convinced that there wasn't a safer window in the world than my love, through which I'd given everything to the person I loved, and I don't want to emphasize 'everything' because I'm not into haggling, I don't give with a view to keep something to myself, all this only occurred to me later, or rather it struck me how quickly love can deteriorate, this is another thing I don't understand, how can something that was so beautiful only yesterday turn so sticky, mouldy and stinky by today, so that by the time you got tired of disappointment, after living together as in a happy marriage devoid of passion, its beauty should suddenly return, albeit passively like in a still life, as if you were looking at snow-covered branches in winter, taking in every single ice flower, every single white tree-trunk and bare tree crown, oh, how beautiful pain without hope can be, this is also happiness of a kind, the happiness that you have had the chance to live, that you can no longer live again, there is nothing to worry about, there are only memories that won't ever run away, on the contrary, you can mould them whichever way you like; twenty-one years ago, when I first flew back to my parents, I understood that I was just as wrong with regard to them as I was with regard to Diego, needless to say, this wasn't much of a consolation, love is not meant to console, not in the least, as long as there's love, the trees are reaching sky-high, when it's over, they fall on their knees, that's it, nothing more, there was nothing to console me, I spent a month in the Seven Turrets and then came here, where I'm writing these words; my poor tearful mother and father saw me off, waving, but refrained from trying to hold me back, and this is to their ultimate credit, they understood that there were no words to suit this situation, and it wasn't up to them to play the role of concerned parents, that was the last time I saw them, half a year later they were both dead, first my father, then my mother, my father had a heart attack, and then my mother drank some poison the next day, why does everything happen with a delay, why does everything arrive with a delay, or in case it happens on time, why does it last so little, I should ask God about this when I see him; in any case, by now I've been living on my parents' faraway estate for three years, a castle I decided to call *Casa del Pasado* to remind me of my beloved Diego, and indeed, what could be a better home for someone who had given up everything, I keep rummaging through my memories, fondling them every so often, I pull their ponytails because memories are always feminine, playful little girls, who might giggle if I tug their hair, then they sulk and move away, and despite me trying to entice them with various cunning tricks, they seem offended, not because of the pain but because they don't understand how I could do this to them, and they are right, whatever happened in whatever manner is not their fault, they weren't the ones who deceived me; still, now that I've stopped flying altogether, I must channel my pain, my bitterness and my disappointment somehow, it would be so nice to have continued to live in love, how happily I'd be on the receiving end of his embraces, kisses, caresses and haughty curtsies before and after a dance, how delightful it would be to see a drop of his favourite red wine shimmer on his lips, and how gladly I'd offer myself up to him with unconditional devotion—but none of this is possible anymore.

There's nothing to be done, I could scream in rage, though I know that there's no one to hear, and no reason to do so, even if God exists, he has better things to do than deal with my love life, mind you, this isn't even a heartbreak but my life, not the agony of a bitch in heat but the awareness that this is all over, that this is a thing of the past and no longer possible, I don't really live anymore only vegetate, eat and drink, wash myself and go to bed because this is the done thing and this is what I was taught to do, but above all, because I don't have the energy to die, I don't have the courage to die like my poor mother did, what death that was, I've seen people die of arsenic and can testify that even survivors don't find this pleasant, in my case, the issue isn't to cope with arsenic-induced spasms, I turn to my memories for help day in, day out, and I hang on to their locks because I realise that they don't really help but only offer what appears to be a help of sorts, and I re-live everything, which is of course fabulous, even though in this way I re-live deception, too, a thousand times stronger despite them being in the past; when events happen for the first time, you can still be hopeful and believe that you are truly alive, but by the time they crystallise like honey, you have lost all hope and find yourself torn between the desire for love and the end of love, neither reversible nor open compromise, and this is the most awful thing in the world for sure.

Besides, love is among the most terrible things possible, we know of no other feeling that can only caress or hit us, its caresses bring to life a new world that in an instant annihilates the previous one, which you had thought would become your shelter for good, you carry the wounds of its flogging until the end of your life, and perhaps there is no other occurrence, process, state or feeling from which one could learn so little, next to nothing to be precise, and for which you embark each time as if there had been no precedent, and from which you could have at least learned that it rarely ends well; it is borderline impossible to maintain mutual thirst, meanwhile you try to forget about it and persuade yourself that you have already done so, while the previous world wildly demands its dues, and by the time you truly live it and immerse yourself into it, love is already over; I haven't had too much experience in this field, and from now on will have even less, but Odile had liberated me to such an extent that I suddenly realised that I was in love with the stableboy, Hans returned my feelings and we found each other as quickly as true lovers tend to do; one time he took me out for a ride, as he had been doing twice a week ever since my eighth birthday, at first, I was accompanied by the equerry, a large grumpy man by the name of Friedrich, even his name was rattling, come, miss, he'd say in his well-meaning manner despite letting out sighs as if he had the worries of the whole wide world on his shoulders, and I only added my own share to this immense pressure, at a time when salvation depended on his contribution; I understood this pain during the time of my love for Hans, I had often seen this same pain on my parents' faces, but didn't understand it back then, and when I did, I just arrogantly pouted my lips, but today, I can understand with my heart, as well as my mind that it's hard to come to terms with your child's striking otherness; Hans was also an only son, just like I was an only daughter to my parents, which meant that they weren't even granted the consolation of having two children of which only one was not to be their spiritual child, both sets of parents had to contend with the horror that they had given life to an alien who can't possibly love them because they can't understand them; besides Hans wasn't even granted the good fortune I was, namely that even though they couldn't understand me and this saddened and frightened them greatly, they nevertheless let me be, Hans' parents, or at least his father Friedrich—seeing in these dour times when men were teaching, fighting, trading, holding mass, who else could possibly destroy the life of children but men, that the destruction of their own children was an outright obligation of good fathers, this could be considered their ultimate task, after all, one has to bear the blame regarding one's offspring—in this way approached the issue, although I'm not sure whether he had actually thought this through, and he reacted in his own way to what he understood it to be, with the thoroughness of a stableman, he'd seriously beat Hans up every single Sunday, he was a god-fearing man who'd listen to mass with beady eyes, one could almost hear the joints of his soul creaking and crackling, he wasn't angry and didn't shout, only punched unconsolably, without sadness, he must have known deep down that everything was in vain, if something doesn't pass, it simply can't be beaten out of someone, but Hans didn't run away, he didn't cry or hit back, he just bent his back and accepted that something was wrong with him and was unsure whether this was his own doing; after a while, we grow together with our fate, I almost burst out laughing when Hans repeated this sentence, I was about to explain to him the time gap between creation and the birth of Jesus, not to mention the issue of Jesus being a decent man, as far as I can see, he wasn't a decent man at all, a decent man doesn't say that happy are those who cry, or that whoever is without sin should be the first to throw a stone, a decent man doesn't charge into a temple to whip the money changers, on the contrary, decent men have their stalls among the money changers, whom Jesus had chased away from God's house, but thankfully I held myself back, there, on Moon-milk meadow, in the purest corner of our love, this explanation would have appeared as a form of aristocratic pride and I'm almost convinced that Hans understood it regardless, without me and my scholarly arguments, he didn't need to be told anything, all one could do to him was hurt him.

He was sixteen and I was a year younger when the moment had finally come, love is really like a skylark, wherever you are, you can hear its wingbeat when the time is right, Hans was quiet the whole day, the polar opposite of his father, a usually cheerful and humorous lad was at this time overwhelmed by sadness, as if unexpectedly covered in puss, his green Slavic eyes turning pensive, and from then on, one couldn't hear a word from him, he just kept silent, at times, we'd ride back to the stables like a two-piece funeral procession, other times, he'd experience the odd in-between instructions, heels down, Katerina, straight back, Katerina, interestingly, he'd never call me 'Miss', and not because he wouldn't want to acknowledge the difference in rank between us, but because I had always been *somebody* for him, a person and not a mere status, so he just carried on with his instructions and then suddenly stopped talking, mid-sentence at times, back then, I thought that this was a consequence of the educational beatings administered by his father, these would have had this impact and tore his life to pieces; it turned out much later that I was seriously mistaken, at first, I tried to get him to talk, but later I realised that it was all in vain, and my good-will was even more harmful because it uprooted him from the silence he absolutely needed *there and then*; love can organise things in such a way that it is left alone when it flies in, it was a resplendent mid-August day when we went for a ride and made it unusually far, later I noticed that we were somewhere in the vicinity of Moon-milk meadow, Hans had discovered it long ago and was very fond of it, relax your hand, Katerina, your wrist shouldn't be tense, he'd repeat while riding, the huge beech trees were shrouding us with their dark shadow and this riding lesson went on for hours despite a degree of tension in the air as Lightning was ambling with me, I became aware that this tension was coming from Hans, it was interesting because one could distinguish between his states of mind, one could have almost erected a fence between his calm joviality and unfathomable silence, this fence, however, was located somewhere beyond good mood, it pulsated in his joviality too, I didn't say a word but waited for something to happen, because I could sense that something was about to happen, and it did; at that point, we were already heading back and as we emerged from under the trees, a storm was approaching, as yet unclear when exactly because we couldn't tell from the position of the clouds, suddenly, I dropped my whip and Hans jumped out of the saddle to pick it up, I could see in his eyes that he was pleased about this minor accident, I knew that what I was waiting for all day was about to happen, he picked the whip up and said, I had asked you to pay attention, and by using the informal address, he signalled his transgression, it was clear to me that with this he had actually transgressed several boundaries at once, and I was right, he jumped into the saddle next to me, grabbed my waist and indicated to Dusk, his magnificent grey Lipizzaner, to follow us, I dug my spurs into Lightning's side and the Arabian thoroughbred shot out at once, racing towards our castle, with Hans's arm on my waist, I could feel the hardness in his jodhpurs, his arms were love itself, I couldn't have cared less if the storm had seized us and whisked us away, out of this world, and I only held Lightning back when I could already make out the very last and furthest turret of our castle.

His father must have got wind of something, and I should give credit to him for this as there must have been some cracks, wounds or sensitivities in this grumpy introvert, the next day Hans was given an additional beating, but he seemed to mind it even less than usual, this time, he wasn't suffering only for his own sake but also for love; such suffering has a hell of a power, not to mention that reciprocated love is heavenly by definition; from then on, we'd ride out every Tuesday and Saturday and would both sit on Lighting, his arms holding me tighter and tighter, I'd been dying to turn towards him, so when he finally kissed my neck after three weeks, I had a feeling that there wasn't anything left for me to experience, of course, I was wrong and there was an awful lot!; led by the eternal rules of love we soon started to play with fire, he'd move back to his horse later and later, our riding lessons were stretching further and further, even my parents started to get suspicious, only Odile was smiling with an omniscient charm until she finally burst out during a geography lesson that the highest peaks were to be found within us, and at times *pas de neige*, so I laughed at her in gratitude because I was desperate for her approval even if I did know that she'd give it to us anyway.

We had to wait half a year until my father went away for a hunt, they had been planning to go hunting for boar in the Stüswardein Mountains for months but somehow it kept being postponed; by this point, I was struggling to

keep Lightning in check, let alone myself, but it
wasn't possible for me to fly since flying requires
a unique combination of tensions, this time Odile
was wrong, although I was in love, I wasn't free
enough to simply fly out of the window, or perhaps I was afraid, yes, it was fear, I don't really
know why I kept avoiding the truth, after all love
is always tied in with fear and wounds, when I saw
my one and only Diego, my heart nearly jumped
out of its place and in this blow, passion and fear
were flashing with lightning, love is pure madness and changes everything, one can't possibly
be in love holding a fan or raising a pinkie finger,
the entire world is coming unhinged, every single
relationship is reassessed; I didn't yet know, and
how could I have possibly known at such a young
age, being almost a child, what I was feeling, and
even if I knew, I wouldn't have admitted to myself
that I was afraid, now I can see clearly that I was
afraid, and it was this fear that hindered me in my
attempts at flying, I had been standing at the wide
open window many times, praying to the moon
to let me fly, how many times I made the decision
that I wouldn't beg anyone, only get on with it and
fly, as Odile had advised me, but it never worked
even though I didn't give up easily, often enough

I'd stand there all night, at times aiding the process with a leap which only led to scratches on
my knees and elbows, I even learned a spell from
Marfa, 'Fly, fly, birds of sky/oh, God, please be our
wise guy/ may love give you wings to fly/and you
devil may you die,' Marfa was George's Russian
wife and my mother's favourite chambermaid,
and now that I am belatedly trying to do justice
to my parents, or at least that modicum of justice
they deserve, I should give credit to my mother
for Marfa, because no matter how unimaginative
this poor George was, always infallible and help-
ful but also extremely dull, so much so that even
his soul had turned into a lackey before he could
have become seriously boring and everyone else
ended up bored to death; or perhaps on the contrary, he could only become such a good valet
because he had long inhabited this role, mind
you, what does 'good' really mean, he wasn't anywhere near what I call a good valet, even servants
are people, first people and then servants, what
kind of a person or individual is the one that can
be so clearly divided in two, a good servant but
an uninteresting person, there is no such thing,
or at least not for me; as for George, it was my
father who insisted on him for reasons unknown

to anyone, seeing that George was a bit much even considering how unimaginative my father was, I should have already been suspicious about this back then, but it's much easier for a child to judge than to understand, in other words, children don't understand nuances, don't have much experience and live in a world of their own, which they can only see in black and white; my father and George had met in the long war, my father had saved his life on the battlefield, where he was wailing after being wounded by a French musketeer, and brought him home, George turned into an excellent domestic, everything was shining bright around my father, his boots, shields, swords, chain-mail, this boring glow had literally gilded my father, I would have never thought that there was such a thing as selfless gold but this was just that; once I couldn't bear it any longer and asked my father what he liked about this man, at first, my father seemed surprised at my question but then a mischievous look appeared in his eyes, something I had never seen before, and he said because he is more of an idiot than me, I should have started my father's examination with this sentence, but I was a child and all I could think was what a hypocrite, he knows this man is stupid and still keeps him in his service, still, this is my father and this is my due.

As I mentioned before, my father was rather keen on order, so he demanded it in all quarters, at the main gate, the castle market, the warehouse, by the gunpower barrels, in the prison as well as the garden, he organised everything according to a system that made the castle look great, this should have made me suspicious, that someone who could so spectacularly turn around a castle that had been exposed to the whim of fate for centuries couldn't be as unimaginative as, to my shame, I had believed him to be for years; Krähe was considered a proper stronghold of robbers, people seemed to have given up on it ever gaining a master who could be taken seriously, but then my father, a margrave, emerged on the scene, and transformed it into one of the empire's glories, its wine was praised far and wide, everybody was dying to visit its garden, seeing that old Wilhelm took better care of it than of his fellow human beings; as it happens, he hated people and unexpectedly confessed this to us himself one Sunday, with the most innocent look on his face, even Odile seemed to be surprised at this, one couldn't have imagined someone more level-headed than old Wilhelm, someone more adjusted or more pleased with the state of the world, someone who liked gladioli or peonies more, his voice continued to be soft but his eyes conveyed a darkness that compelled us to make ourselves scarce at once without saying a word; to cut a long story short, my father was indeed fond of order, but as George's case demonstrates, he could also find it rather amusing, even if he tried to keep this mainly to himself.

My mother also attended the hunt, the lady of the Stüswardein castle was counting the days until her arrival, and I could have gone with them, too, but I had decided years ago not to attend any aristocratic gathering; I was still a child when, despite my objections, they took me to Lifstein Manor, the estate of my father's elder brother, Count von Purtzenwald, it was the fiftieth birthday of my brave uncle, so he thought it appropriate to invite his entire extended family, then equally appropriate to order some poor sod to drink champagne, and once everyone was suitably merry, to pour the contents of his tobacco case into a large glass and make the poor man gulp it down, with a view to find out what would happen, soon enough he could see this indeed, the poor man's temperature shot up and within the span of forty-eight hours, he gave up his ghost amidst the most terrible agony; I found all this deeply revolting and while those in attendance were also horrified by this cruel prank, they seemed to mainly scold the dead man, implying that this wasn't the done thing in polite society, as I went up to my uncle, my face red with rage, he first tried to deride all this, but when he realised that I'm not someone to see the funny side of this, his smile vanished from his face and all he said was: the man was given the last rites, he seemed to show true repentance, and when I then started to scream and shout that this was nice enough but had nothing to do with my uncle, this wasn't his repentance but that of the dead man, he just kept repeating: the man was given the last rites and he showed true repentance; firstly, at that point I understood, that no matter what one might say, for these people a case of death is just another form of amusement, like riding or hunting, secondly, I swore an oath that I wouldn't go anywhere with my parents again, and informed them of this decision straightaway, the faces of my stunned mother and even more stunned father gave away that in their view this minor accident was a much needed boost to a gathering heading to a low point, and all I did was ruin the best party in the world.

Incidentally, it's interesting how diverse people's reactions can be when it comes to bad jokes, even death, depending on the perpetrator; as I remember this, all I can do is be ashamed, but at the same time, after all these years and after the most awful love story of my life, I am proud of what my Diego told me during our potentially most passionate night, between embraces; oh, I should have really sensed that the end was nigh, one can only go downhill from here, but people cannot pre-empt things, this is why they are *people* and not some snow-covered cliff, because they immerse themselves into life, what would otherwise become of love if not an endless lookout as to when one's beloved might leave; meanwhile, there is fear burning in your bones, this is why you're offering up your lap, let him thrust and thrust, at least he might love you while he's harder than hard, this is also among the wonderful horrors of love that heaven is as hard as it can possibly get; Diego told me that during his vagabond years, still back in his country, he joined a plot against the king and the lord of Castellor, the cold and arrogant Count Luna invited him to his castle, after

a peaceful discussion in the armoury, one of the
gentlemen in attendance, Count Manrico started
to brag about his sword, what a fabulous weapon,
there's no armour that it couldn't penetrate, no
helmet that it couldn't crush, until my Diego lost
his temper, goodness, his bright green eyes sparkling in the dark, and with the gallantry of a dance
master asked to inspect the sword, he swished it a
few times and then abruptly thrust it into Count
Manrico himself, who instantly gave up his ghost
with eyes wide with bewilderment, meanwhile,
my Diego took a bow in front of the gentlemen
frozen to death, this is indeed an excellent sword,
he blurted out with a mix of rage and joy from the
corner of his mouth, and took his leave.

IV

And yet, I'm still not ready to write about him.
Today, I have to write about Hans and about
the fact that my father had finally left home, on
such occasions my mother would stay in her
room and ask Marfa to serve her breakfast there;
in this angry, or shall I say frustrated, phase of
my childhood, when I thought I was the most
miserable creature on earth because I was the
only one with such impossible parents, back
then I thought that my mother would destroy
this poor woman, as I said before, Marfa hailed
from Russia and her face was just as hard to read
as this enormous barbaric empire, her skin was
still milky white despite being around forty at
the time when I was hoping to experience love
with Hans, or to be precise, that thing I thought
to be love with all the bitter passion of my fif-
teen years; goodness, how we tend to despise our
first object of desire once we meet our true love,
instead of writing treatises about various princely

ruses, Italian and other scholars and philosophers should dedicate their attention to love, in this way they'd be able to shed light on many more events, find out a lot more about mankind and, on the whole, be of much more immediate use, although, who knows, perhaps the only thing they'd find out is that nothing can be known for certain, Marfa's skin and sea-grey eyes were the most obvious proof that time is being experienced from within, according to our personal laws, the laws of our own soul, and this has nothing to do with actual time-measuring devices which pretend that everybody is subject to the exact same temporal rules and that everybody's time passes at the same pace; I had once actually seen such an ingenious device at the magnificent castle of the Prince-elector of Bundenfalz, I was invited by his wife, my beloved aunt Jadwiga Komorowska, who basically commanded my mother to introduce her daughter to high society at their annual February ball, my mother was only her niece but this wasn't an offer she could refuse, I was sixteen at the time, a year earlier I was still panting after Hans, and then with him, but at that ball in Bundenfalz I had to conceal this side of myself; we arrived with three chest-loads of fancy garments, my parents, fully aware of my weirdness, to put it mildly, were already terrified that I'd bring shame on them in some way, to be honest, I was also experiencing a tenseness of sorts, it's not easy to always be the weird one, all this questioning and disapproval is a terrible burden to bear and at times, one snaps under its weight; I got there as if I myself was watching this sixteen-year-old girl with suspicion, seeing that she had never managed to do anything properly, like everyone else, wondering what could she do differently at this masked ball, Countess Komorowska, however, had immediately seen through me: tell me, sister, why haven't you introduced this grand duchess to us before, and I knew at once what this gently melodic word meant and took an immediate liking to the Countess, being able to sense that she had only thrown in her apparent harshness to ensure that my parents bring me to the ball; from then on, she didn't really have much time for them, she grabbed my hand as if she were about to drown and my hand represented the only chance for salvation, and dragged me along the corridors illuminated by torches, every so often ghosts would also appear carrying torches, but we just kept marching on until we made it to a room, no idea where, with nothing in sight except for the gruesome walls, and in front of us, a weird contraption, rectangular at the bottom and triangular at the top, with a gigantic golden knob in the middle of the triangle, on which there was some kind of a pendulum, swinging from right to left, inside the triangle there was a circle with some numbers, and inside the circle, two elongated shapes, the longer currently positioned on the number six and the shorter on the number eight, twenty to six, the Countess informed me, and sensing that I didn't understand what she meant, she added that this something was a device to measure time, soon it will be six o'clock, so we were just standing in that bare room in front of this golden object, one could cut the silence to pieces, but then we both burst out laughing at the same time, with an elemental force that shook even this unusual device and made me realize that my mother's aunt was a grand duchess herself.

As soon as this silence had come to an end, Jadwiga held out her hand and grabbed mine with her trademark gentle resolve, this frightened me, could it be that she isn't a grand duchess after all and will start lecturing me on the emotional connection between us, I was already gearing up for

disappointment, on account of my parents, I was
very advanced when it came to disappointment,
but my mother's aunt wasn't about to lecture me,
she didn't say a word only looked into me, I can't
put this any other way, she looked at me, scrutinising me for a moment and then nodding and
letting go of my hand, I could swear that in that
moment she would have been able to tell even
the name of my sometime-lover, goodness, how
distant this love seemed already, despite having
been the ultimate wonderfully hard-earned real-
ity only here months earlier, a steaming hot lawn
on Moon-milk meadow, but on this occasion at
Bundenfalz, there was no time to swear because
all of a sudden, we could hear the sound of mon-
strous merriment, as if pearls had been cast in
front of swine, we yanked the door open right
away and started running through various corridors well-known to Jadwiga, I didn't have a clue
about where these corridors might lead, but I had
no intention of running in any other direction;
when we finally got to the castle's grand hall, we
were met with a horrific sight, all the guests were
standing around a dubious figure, some *chevalier*
by the name of Zeingalt or such-like, I refused to
remember it but I deliberately remembered the

little girl, Katharina Blum was the name of the
poor creature, the eight-year-old daughter of the
estate steward, whom this widely travelled man,
who had obviously trampled on many women,
was pinching while holding a restraining grip
on her and growling with vile depravity every
time the little girl cried out in pain, blood was
already spurting under the nails of this bastard
as he kept squeezing the girl's round cheeks, with
those in attendance naturally taking the side of
this beast; I was desperately hoping that my parents wouldn't be present though I knew that they
were, most probably roaring with laughter like
everyone else, for a moment, I had even spotted
my mother's cowardly gaze as she looked at me in
fear, my father didn't yet notice me, only after the
following pinch when he cast a part authoritative
and part suppliant look at me; the Prince-elector
was personally in charge of the fun and Zeingalt
appeared to be watching his reactions closely, as
soon as he received permission, he pecked yet
again at the bleeding angelic face; I wanted to
charge at them but Jadwiga got ahead of me, I
don't know where she got this whip from, but by
the time I noticed it, she was already brandishing
it with her cheeks aflame, swishing it with the full

force of her rage, like an amazon, lashing it first at her husband's and then at the knight's face, the guests could only rattle and shriek, frozen with fear, some of the more sensitive souls, who moments earlier found pleasure in witnessing a child's agony, fainted at the sight of such brutality, I remember thinking that quite a few people would probably be horrified at the sight of Jesus whipping the money changers, the Prince-elector touched his face and as he felt blood, his gaze flared up, compared to Jadwiga's volcanic fire, however, his was just about enough to fuel a fireplace, meanwhile, Zeingalt let out an odd moan and muttered under his breath, before he made his way out of the hall at the same time as his despicable master, albeit in a different direction.

Jadwiga and I dashed over to Katharina at once, my compassion additionally heightened by us sharing the same name, I made a bandage from my dress with which to dress her injured face, meanwhile, Jadwiga was trying to calm her down, stroking her until this angelic creature had stopped shedding tears and her being was emanating an ethereal glow, the glow of all-forgiveness which I knew I'd never partake of, after she had duly thanked us for our help, she said her goodbyes,

following which Jadwiga signalled to the guests
to start dispersing, too; as my mother and father
also made their way out, the valets brought in our
travel chests and the lady of the house placed her
hands on my head and held them there for a little
while, then bid us farewell, we all kept silent in the
carriage, without saying a single word until we got
home, I was kneeling with my back to my parents
the whole journey and kept looking out of the
window, my mother made a single attempt at tugging my arm to make me face them, but I turned
away so stubbornly that she gave up trying again;
as our carriage was racing across the Schoeblin-
gen meadow, the moon was shining particularly
bright just as an angel suddenly winged its way
over the landscape, as if slicing the moon in two;
my first thought was about what time that weird
contraption could possibly show, my second that
we couldn't be far from Bundenfalz, and the next
day, after a part wonderful and part excruciating
experience and a terrible journey, I was so restless
that I could barely listen to Odile, this continued
onto the third day and for further days, until one
evening a letter arrived from Jadwiga, in which
she informed us with her trademark warmth that
Katharina Blum had died that very night, unable

to cope with her humiliation, and was buried the next day; the Prince-elector offered a tidy sum to her parents, who were most undeserving of their beautiful child, to this day, I'm not sure why I was crying and whom I was in fact mourning, Jadwiga or Katharina, unaware that I would have plenty of opportunities for crying in the future, and even then, there wouldn't be anyone I could expect any help from.

Death, however, was a great lesson, akin to most of my other formative experiences, such as teenage and then adult love, it changed my life for good and I understood that angels die, too, there is no place for them here on earth, beauty has a degree of vulnerability that doesn't belong with the mean and small-minded games of mere mortals; back then, I thought it did, what else could I have thought at the age of sixteen, I saw myself as an exception and didn't include my own person among those to be blamed; I only realised after my frantic love for Diego and our devastating break-up that one shouldn't judge anyone on this earth unless one was prepared to join the accused, this isn't your average court, where the judge can just go home and smoke their well-deserved meerschaum pipe while the executioner chops the head of the convict off, the axe swooshing and the guilty head flying off; the sheer fact that I didn't die young like Katharina, after being tormented to death by that monster Zeingalt, is enough of an accusation, after all, who else could be tormented to death and turned into a martyr if not those who don't belong among us, and who are the tormentors, if not those who are one of us by definition, that child was the embodiment of innocence, she had known no sin *in any shape or form*, she didn't experience pleasure writhing under men, she was nothing but a victim, while I was a participant, I had well and truly participated in everything that happened to me, and regardless of whether I'm proud or ashamed of what had happened, I know that things end up intertwined, it's not possible to draw a line between commendable and disgraceful facts, there are nuances, of course, one is a bit closer to the former and the other to the latter, but where would I be in a black-and-white world, nowhere, Katharina, on the other hand, is all white because she didn't get to live past that invisible and clearly undefinable age barrier after which one is no longer entitled to see the world in black and white; I shouldn't have been entitled, either, but my stupid arrogance made me believe that I had the right to do this and to exercise a continuous contempt with which I treated my parents and into which I immersed myself despite clear warnings; I remember my surprise when Odile took their side, this isn't quite the right term, Odile didn't stand with anything or anyone, Odile *was simply being relational*, and now, when I'm trying to tidy up my life by way of writing these words, even though I practically have no life, I realise that this is the very point, goal, intent and essence of humour, being relational without judging anyone, keeping out while also keeping in, as one should; we were walking in the woods back then, and I blew up when my father had chased Marfa away from my mother, out of my sight, you Russian witch, he shouted while my mother just kept silent, I was outraged by the behaviour of both and could only croak in my anger, how could somebody be like this, like a common stableboy, and how could somebody just keep silent as if they were mute; *à quoi bon*, Odile mused, she could come up with a *comparaison* for everything, and carried on, *à quoi bon*, everyone is so *commun*, even yesterday's *amour*, at that point, I felt ashamed and felt that Hans wasn't just any old stableboy, but how could I have set apart the stableboy in him from the prince he had been for me on Moon-milk meadow, there was no way I could have defended myself from myself, because Odile had already leapt away, swallowed by the woods, while I was swallowed by shame, mind you, this shame didn't last long and, above all, didn't soak into my soul, it was only a momentary embarrassment like when a parent scolds a child, it didn't lead anywhere and soon enough, I was croaking yet again, by then already out of earshot of Odile's generously rolled R's, too.

As I have mentioned already, she resigned her soul to God during the great plague, God had taken her despite Marfa's best efforts, back then, I was struggling to believe in God, all I did was shake my fists at the vacuous heavens, the question why, why, why kept *rattling* in me, in fact, it was tearing, ripping and mauling me apart; why does God have to interfere when one finally meets someone who's not only special but also living in the same place, with whom one can both talk and stay silent together, because they observe silence in the same manner of frantic love, why does God have to interfere and take away the only glimmer of hope; from one day to the next, lumps appeared on her neck, armpits and other more private locations, on the last night of her life I decided that I was no longer interested in interdictions, I wasn't even interested in my own life, perhaps because I was hoping that this selfless flaring of love might help with keeping her on this side, I dashed to her room and reduced Marfa to silence with a single glance, even my parents, who came to witness the last rites, refrained from saying anything, by then she was in such horrific pain that she attempted twice to jump out of the window, *la mort est un oiseau énorme,* she panted, burning hot like a furnace and spitting blood, *maintenant, je sais c'est l'infini,* she sobbed, oh, if at least this didn't happen; Marfa looked into the void, I imagine she must have been consumed by guilt since none of her hidrotic and febrifugal teas helped, be it Benedictine grass, thyme, black elder, peppermint, I did realise that this wasn't Marfa's fault yet I was still cross with her and couldn't understand why she didn't try one of her spells, whenever I asked her to do so, this wise-woman just shook her head, and in case I asked her why, seeing that she knew countless such spells and incantations, she responded with a categorical no; Father Brouillard was the priest who administered the last rites, who else, so I couldn't help thinking that even on her last journey she was accompanied by a boring lot, what could I do but dismiss all this with a wave, and just stood there with my parents next to her bed, they were praying and I was crying on the inside, with my lips tightly drawn, and then Odile suddenly sat up in her bed, lifted by some unearthly power, she looked around as if desperately seeking someone, I came closer assuming that she must have been looking for me, and indeed, her tearful eyes lit up when she saw me, Katerina, life is beautiful because death is on its way, she said squirming on feverish waves, but I didn't give credence to her despite the fact that there was little time for doubt, because next, Odile pushed Brouillard away, fell back and breathed her last; that very moment, her face started to show acquiescence, gleaming the whole night through up until she was placed in a coffin, after which the coffin was gleaming, too, at least as long as I could see it, because I wasn't allowed to attend her funeral despite my persistent begging and stamping my feet, I managed to keep her deathbed but this was all I could obtain, you are my daughter and you must live!, my mother cried obstinately, and now I can see that this would have been yet another opportunity for me to get to understand her.

At this point, however, I wasn't yet prepared to be understanding, and with the passage of time I increasingly think that insightful understanding goes hand in hand with cluelessness, when you are young, you are anything but clueless, you need time to comprehend that there are countless nuances to things, events, phenomena and of course people, and that even beauty is under the influence of these; what's more, it seems as if beauty was actually attracting these subtle differences, there is no beauty without some degree of mystery, and there is nothing more mysterious than what is visible, touchable, enjoyable and yet incomprehensible, beauty is that thing which no doubt *exists* and well, what do you mean well?, which changes one's life, it is something that bursts into our destiny like doom and snatches us from the waters of indifference like a white whale, you're really rooting for it to show up yet you're also afraid of it, as you are afraid of that whale called Morgan which cruises around the coasts of Japan and spouts a white cross-shaped foam, it's obvious that mere description cannot give us an idea of all this, the whale isn't to be found where we see these lumps and bumps or other similar protrusions, and I'm convinced that this white cross-shaped blow also belongs to the realm of fairy tales, but what else would the purpose of fairy tales be if not to help people tuck their teeth into something they don't and can't understand, so in this respect, the white cross is truer than truth because it conveys something that couldn't be conveyed in any other way, and it makes it crystal clear that beauty is cruel and doesn't care about anything except itself, and that love is none other than the encounter of two people who chanced upon each other at the same time, they found one another attractive and paid no heed to anything apart from this feeling which was feeding on its own self until it was no longer able to satisfy itself and ended up toppling the very world it had previously created.

Another reason why I couldn't show more sympathy was that barely a minute after Odile passed away, Father Brouillard had already gotten carried away with his reaching, at first, I didn't even register what was happening, I was completely immersed in pain, and in my selfishness, I could only think of myself, wondering what would happen to me without her, without her laughter, her typically French rolled R's, her wisdom and her freedom, it took a while until I heard the unpleasant voice of this baritone, as he was going through the number of deaths around our castle, 'so far, more than forty people died in Mähnedorf in a week', he then cast a stern look on me to justify my parents' unflinching decision, 'no-one feels more sorry for them than I, and I regret Odile Rouge-Gorge perhaps even more, although there is no difference between them in front of God', this made me burst out in laughter, so far I didn't realize that even Odile's last name was basically robin in French; my parents immediately looked at me in dismay and Brouillard paused reproachfully for a moment, in response to which I shouted: The hypocrite is known by his actions, not by his clothes! I don't know why this came to my mind, but my mother reacted with dropping her head to her chest, it looked as if someone was tugging at my father's moustache and Marfa's fiery eyes were merging with Odile's halo, as for me, I simply bolted out of this unbearable situation and from this room where, for the first time, I had lost someone I truly loved.

Soon enough, I had the opportunity to get used to loss, because in no time I had to lose Hans, too, not before falling in love with him and giving myself to him though, this happened about six months before Odile's death, when we hadn't as much as heard about the plague, let alone suspected the sort of changes it would bring to our lives, I guess I was attracted to him with curiosity and passion in equal measure, because the night when my father had finally went away, I waited until the very last hoofbeat had died away and could only hear something that I was unable to decipher in my ears, with a torch I then signalled to this fairy tale stableboy, who was already waiting for my cue, shivering with excitement, even though he must have known that in no time he'd set the sky aflame, after all he was the one to saddle the horses with which my father and his retinue had departed for the great hunt where the lord of the manor, an exceptional warlord and, according to hearsay, also a poet, had been killed by a boar, rumour had it, and I could see in my father's eyes that this was true, that a gun had actually put an end to his life, but they blamed the boar, people can hardly ever live, love, make mistakes or sin in an unadulterated fashion, one always needs something, such as God, religion, a king, a ruler or love, in order to conduct one's business which is life with a clean conscience, because we lend ourselves to slogans, so in the end slogans will constitute our very life: honesty—virtue, restraint—purity, principles—love; at that time, however, I was still far too naïve, young and naïve, and with all the might of my ineptitude I wanted to gain some experience, I was literally suffering that I hadn't yet been given the chance and it didn't even occur to me to ask myself whether other girls of my age had gotten it, people are selfish and stupid, my body was craving for him, for Hans, I hadn't yet met any other men I could consider, only arrogant and vulgar peasant lads, whose very humility felt offensive, besides Hans had offered me his body many times by then, whenever we were riding back home, sitting together in the saddle, he'd hug me so tight that it hurt and I could feel his sweet lap, I loved and wanted his hardness and was pleased about the pain despite Marfa's warning, she had spotted everything with her sharp green eyes, even the truth, and one evening, just as I had jumped off the horse, she suddenly came to my room and told me that not all kinds of pain were the same, Missy, she was the only one to call me this, to everyone else I was Miss Katerina and to Odile, simply Katerina, our body parts are extremely capable of changing place, she added and then vanished, as quickly as she had appeared, and I was left there with a sentence I didn't quite understand, even though I did understand the point she was trying to make.

That said, understanding in itself is to no avail, the time of suffering will still come and *then* you will definitely understand everything, that day, we rode out to Moon-milk meadow, Hans had given this name to the area seeing that he had already discovered it three years earlier, he'd regularly flee there from his father's rage, at first, only after major beatings, because, as he had later told me, he had made a promise early on that he'd cope with the beatings even if that was the last thing he did, I asked about the reason for these beatings in vain, at such times, he'd just adopt a gloomy look, his face would get literally shielded and he'd change the subject or just carry on talking but under no circumstances about *that*, but about something entirely different, nobody could forbid him to go wherever he wanted after the beatings, he continued, at first, he'd just walk aimlessly under the giant trees and wouldn't cry, pain is like a church service, not needed but compulsory, this sounded like a contradiction, as if he had come up with it deliberately to enchant me, how stupid we are, how arrogant and selfish, as if everything had been revolving around me, as if a boy who was being beaten like a dog had wanted me in between the lashings administered by way of a hazelnut stick, but most probably he did indeed want me and when he realised that this wasn't impossible, he got all the more keen to get me, one shouldn't sweep trust away, this was another outcome of my unfortunate relationship with my parents, the only person I trusted was Odile, because one simply couldn't not trust her, Hans, on the other hand, wasn't trustworthy even when I thought I was in love with him, in any case, I couldn't care less about these pre-prepared sentences, all I wanted was his body, by then I had already asked Odile what it was like, and resented her that she didn't seem to want to respond, *l'amour*, she said, *c'est comme un* door that suddenly *deplier* in front of you, and you can't move away from under it, I had to laugh, she wasn't quite clear about grammatical cases but she immediately realised that she had made a mistake, this time she didn't laugh as she'd normally do, instead she looked rather sad, *l'amour, ma petite Catherine, pas de tout* easy, and this truly shook me, until this point she had been pronouncing my name in such a perfect German accent that not even Hans could say it any better, this time, however, I could tell that she was using the French variant deliberately, and this made me understand that love wasn't some game, where the losers get a concern and the winners can run home with a commendation.

Odile had often written me up when she felt I was cheeky and she must have often had this impression, I had many bad days since I had become a woman, a woman in the true sense of the word, not in the sense that I was born one, everybody was aware of that, but in that I got my first period, this was a secret Marfa had warned me about, Marfa somehow managed to put in an appearance whenever there was some mystery looming on the horizon, on that particular August night, a huge red raven had appeared at my window, I was restless and couldn't sleep, walking up and down in my room, I was fourteen and there were many things I was unable to understand, this even less than others, what could possibly make me get out of bed when I was trying to lie down, what was chasing my bones, my room was just a set and I wasn't really walking but running up and down, my body was fire and water all at once, in flames yet billowing at the same time, I couldn't make sense of this, I was panting and sweating, hurting all over, my breasts were hard as a rock, my groins aflame, but I still couldn't understand any of this and was waiting for a clue, so I welcomed this raven as a bearer of a solution, not as a bird foreboding death, of which I had heard enough by then, in any case, this was a *red* raven, not a black one, what could it possibly bring?, I didn't know, but whatever it did, it was here, perching on my windowsill, and as it was preening its feathers, I noticed something hanging from its beak, well, even if this bird is no bearer of a solution, it had actually brought me *something*, I carefully stepped a little closer, I could see that it was a daring bird, and what's more important, that it had a mission, it had come for me, it wouldn't fly away, I carefully held out my hand, its wings and unusual body accepted my touch, I moved my fingers in the direction of its beak, and in no time, I was in possession of that something, I held it up and it was a piece of ruby, a beautifully glittering gem, it drew my gaze in but out of the blue, I could feel that my hands had gotten wet, the ruby had trickled away from my hand and the red raven flew away cawing; I didn't even have time to come back to my senses when I suddenly felt a twinge, at first, I didn't understand, this was an upshot of earlier moments of not understanding, but I had no time to ponder on this, the twinge was pouring out of me, and although nobody had told me what to do in such situations, I had seen the odd maid giggle and swish past while bleeding, without having the slightest idea why that was, my instinctive otherworldly reaction was that this must be because they were *girls*, this of course isn't much of an insight, this is practically nothing, yet this time, I did know what I had to do, I ripped a piece of fabric from my petticoat and placed it by this pulsating absence, which for me was actually something, even when it wasn't pulsating, and I sensed that I had instantly become a new person, at the beginning of a new life, with novel and unpredictable things looming on the horizon.

The next morning, I spotted that same ruby on Marfa's neck, and she greeted me with a conspiratorial wink.

VI

The pain I felt when I gave myself to Hans was similar to this, by the time we made it to Moon-milk meadow we were already neighing like horses, but still, my considerate love made sure to unload the food basket he had prepared so we didn't die of hunger by the next morning, I was soaking wet, as if I had been rolling in the dewy grass all day, it was a magnificent early autumn night, the moon was pouring its sheer white light as if it was indeed made of milk, Hans tied Lightning and Dusk to a tree, and headed awkwardly towards me, I didn't just wait there, either, and by the end we were both running towards each other, the horses were nickering, the trees protruding from the ground like boars keeping watch, and all I wanted was some tusk, Hans grabbed me and held me close to his body, I could feel his groin, his hardness and wetness, he took me to the middle of the meadow and quickly removed the muslin scarf from my breasts, he started to kiss my nipples but could hardly control himself, I was able to sense that his hardness was hurting him, I was waiting and waiting, kissing him wherever I could, but this wasn't enough for me either, until he finally dipped his magnificent tusk in me, or rather what I had found magnificent up to that point, because that very moment it felt as if I had been torn apart and ripped in two, my entire body felt numb and I started to bleed between my thighs, I cried out in fear, I must have looked like that miserable sod who had fallen off the roof of our mansion while doing some timber work, a muffled wail, everybody had dashed outside, so I also ran towards the crowd, people let me and my terrified parents pass through until we got to the poor man lying petrified on the ground, as if he was fully aware that what was about to come was worse than death, he had fallen on his back, people were whispering in commiseration, and right now I would have looked just like that had anybody seen me, I threw Hans off me and immediately took flight, I was tricked, I said to myself, despite not being able to pin down who could have actually done such a thing, perhaps I tricked myself, but meanwhile, I kept soaring higher and higher, the sullen trees looked like needles and the moon like a cymbal, I found everything fake, what did they do to me, Moon-milk, seeing that I had to take to splitting the sky, if only I could really split it in two, and barely noticed that a red bird was flying next to me, for a lap, then another, and finally a third, and when it realised that this wasn't enough for me, it landed on the edge of the moon and just watched as I continued to fly onwards and upwards.

I have no idea how long I had been flying until my pain subsided, and together with it, me too, in any case for quite some time, I understood or rather sensed that this pain was the price of future pleasures to come, without this, those pleasures couldn't happen, and that Hans was not responsible for my pain, I would have felt the same no matter who had taken from me what had just been taken, and let's not forget about this word, either, this 'finally' says an awful lot in itself, I wanted to lose it, after all, a stableboy wouldn't have been able to take it without my consent, so I shouldn't behave as if I wasn't in my right mind, even though love in itself is a mindless invention, otherwise one couldn't feel it or engage in it, not even in front of oneself, but then at least I should be consistent with the mind of love, I should somehow

placate Hans, the poor sod can't grasp what had
happened, and in case he can, he certainly can't
understand why I flew away, not to mention that I
had shown my true colours, but then again what is
love if not the revelation and sharing of secrets, as
I kept mulling this over and was approaching the
meadow, I noticed something strange, a wolf was
sniffing around looking larger in the moonlight
than the average wolf, more like the specimen
whose fur my father had once proudly brought
home, I wasn't able to properly assess all this from
above, so I settled on a nearby tree and continued
watching from there, the wolf urinated on a tree-
trunk and then went up to our food basket, but it
had barely stuck its nose into it when it came to a
halt under the very tree where I had been hiding,
it turned its huge snout towards the moon and
started howling, with bitterness and desperation
as if being lovelorn, it was getting close to daybreak, all my limbs had gotten numb and I had
even dozed off by the time it finished, but Hans
was nowhere to be seen, no matter how keen I
was to find him, Lightning and Dusk were still
relatively calm, they were exceptionally obedient
horses, I said to myself and was even proud of
them, but then the wolf suddenly finished and

vanished into the woods, at this point I came down only to find Hans already standing behind me, where have you been?, I asked, but he dismissed my question with a wave of his hand, let's go, he said half-heartedly, and we duly started off on our way.

The next evening, it was he who asked for forgiveness, crying, he couldn't cope with having hurt me so much, but I should understand that he was only…, but before he could have continued, I placed my index finger on his lips and started to circle it, and with my other hand, I was caressing his groin, I could see in his eyes that he was surprised, this wasn't what he expected, he was expecting something quite different, something really feminine; every time I reflect on this scene, I brood over the fact that he had basically insulted me twice over, on the one hand, why did he think that I was like *other* women, on the other, how could he know what women were like anyway, after all, one needs some experience for such observations, how could he possibly compare me to anyone if not by having had similar experiences with them; I had in fact seen him a few times with Anne, George and Marfa's beautiful daughter of my age, in whom her father's reserve and her mother's witchcraft had merged in a uniquely inspiring fashion, the two of them were occasionally to be found together in various hiding places, but as soon as they noticed me, they'd move on, billowing continuously, I had caught sight of the odd kiss and even some panting on one occasion, something between moaning and crying, but I was unable to verify what was happening despite my best efforts at peeking in the direction of this sound, Anne had suddenly appeared from an entirely different location, she was truly beautiful, almost unashamedly beautiful considering her rank, or rather lack thereof, her Slavic mightiness, which was anything but softness, the Slavs aren't soft at all, yet they are aware that there's so many of them and they are roaming such large territories that they could even afford to be soft, this self-confidence styled as softness was demonically complimented by English discipline, and from her blinding white skin and the blond waterfall of her hair, there emerged her deep brown, wounded gaze, that could also be defiant at times, she looked at me with scorn, this servant, the servant daughter of servants, as if she wanted to say, you are peeking after us in vain, miss, so I dashed back to Odile, crying, but Odile just wrote me up again, you again *diffère*, Katerina, she could see that I was inconsolable and yet she didn't have mercy on me, she asked all sorts of questions about European geography, perhaps she wanted to say that love isn't everything, or perhaps that one should beware of love, because some shadow was always showing on her face; today, I'd say she looked as if the bird of happiness had been slipping away and this was showing on her face, back then, I wasn't so poetic or perhaps so empty, so full of so many absences, I actually wanted to ask her what sort of shadow it was, but she died.

That night, when I was peeking after Anne and Hans in vain, I suddenly heard some mischievous fluttering by my window, at first, I didn't want to believe my ears, I put it down to being half-asleep, but it didn't go away and kept fluttering until I got out of bed and went to my window, Marfa and Anne were standing in the air, or to be precise, they were sitting or rather looked like they were sitting on something, they indicated that I should join them but I didn't understand what they meant, at which point Marfa simply pulled me out of my room, gently as if I were featherlight, and I felt just like that, hovering and capable of anything without wings or any other help, we were hovering and gliding for ages, and I didn't feel tired until we got to the top of a mountain, I have never seen this wild black cliff before, I wouldn't have expected to hover until we got to some unknown place, but it didn't really matter, this is what happened, we landed and they led me to the opening of a cave guarded by three monkeys, a single glance of Marfa's made them let their pointy tails down, we stepped into the dark and saw a large cauldron on a low fireplace being stirred by some figures, I could sense that this wasn't what this place was about, this was just the set, the props, so I was waiting for my eyes to get used to the mist inside, when I finally turned my head, I could see why they had taken me here, in the middle of the space there were three witches, whom I didn't know, when I got back home at dawn with a roaring sound in my ears, I had to laugh at my presumption that I should know every witch; I didn't have time to worry about such things though, Marfa and Anne had already moved beyond the three hags, to an area where, in a staggering cascade of rays, there was a soul sitting, with only a pair of green eyes shining bright, I can't put this any other way, Marfa and Anne led me to this creature and instinctively stepped back, the eyes started to scrutinise me, looked straight inside me, *ermosachiha*, the creature whispered in a matter-of-fact tone, then stared at me some more and I could feel its gaze penetrate me all the way to my spine, *chihainsegua*, it whispered again, *chihainfelis*, it whispered for the third time, and then Marfa and Anne came up to me, bowed and led me away, we left the cave and flew back to where we had come from, which had now seemed just as unusual and unworldly as our nighttime adventure; back home, as I laid my head on my pillow, I fell asleep at once and the next day, I started begging Odile to teach me some Spanish, she must speak this language, I have no idea how I realised that what I had heard was Spanish, but I made a note of what the eyes told me in my diary; Odile, however, just kept shaking her head with a sadness on her face that I had only seen a single time since then, it must have been at this moment that she decided she should catch the plague.

VII

I know it must sound strange, but during my whirlwind years in Syladia, when I was the wife of Prince Nicolaus and also the lover of my divine Diego, who occupied my every thought and whom I wanted every single minute of the day even though my body was supposed to behave like a princess, Count Ioannes, whom I had hated as much as I hated meat with cabbage, a favourite of the local lords around there, called me a depraved female beast in his autobiography, despite the fact that he was nothing but a rat himself, a lurking busybody, a snooping piece of shit, who had also been instrumental in my separation from my Diego, according to Count Ioannes, therefore, I wasn't fit for a princess, I'm not really disputing this, since I had never really been interested in this role, I can't find words to describe how boring it was, besides, I was unable to love Prince Nicolaus, either, even though he wasn't a bad man as such, only had a strong body

odour; during these years in Syladia, I had met a
wonderful man, a certain Pasha Hayvan, the wise
Turkish ambassador, I can't remember how this
had come about but one day we had just suddenly
found ourselves strolling in the Princely garden,
a place everyone talked about with great pride
despite it being a lot smaller than our garden,
where you could easily spend half a day, not just
a meagre few hours, and where we used to have
my riding lessons when I was younger, here, by
the time you'd get in the mood you'd have to turn
around and leave; this time, I was taking a walk
with Pasha Hayvan and our conversation had
suddenly sparkled, oh, how I missed this spark
in my poor husband, or to be precise, I didn't
miss it, it would have killed me, but still, on a
human level, he couldn't represent more in my
eyes than utter boredom even though everyone
kept singing his praises, I literally cheered up
when I had once caught him as he was having
his favourite dog, Outlaw, lick his dangly bits, he
immediately jumped up, no matter how heavily
I protested, and chased the poor creature away,
trying to explain in his embarrassment that his
bits were hurting him; this Pasha Hayvan had
just arrived around that time from a Languedoc

recently devastated by the plague, he told me and even illustrated his point by drawing in the sand with a stick, that the plague is a spiritual disease, you see, Princess, may Allah send some beautifully scented roses above your head to protect you from the scorching sun, you see, the plague never tends to spread further north, so I'd like to know which *purely* bodily illness chooses its victims, the answer is that there is no such illness, and it was at this point that I realised that this man was right, the plague does actually handpick people, so I continued my train of thought and stopped paying attention to poor Pasha Hayvan, who resented this a little but what could he do, that's human nature, if the other's passion is only good to fuel yours but not enough to make the two of them stick together, you get bored, passion isn't an act of charity, if this claim about choice is true, then this means that the plague can also be chosen so to speak, it can be asked to be yours and to take you away, this conversation had instantly opened my eyes, I understood Odile's gloom, her strange words about love, her sadness at times when she had seemingly no reason to be sad, I shooed the disappointed Pasha Hayvan away, together with my nine ladies-in-waiting, who had always been a nuisance and this had only got worse lately, and there, under the chestnuts of the Princely garden, I well and truly let out a last tear for Odile, because grief is also a duty of sorts that one cannot neglect, weeping is a custom while love is not, or if it is, it's a custom that cannot do without a personal touch, that special something which turns everything into beautiful horror.

I sobbed and wept, grieving for everything that Odile had and could have represented, for everything that I could have become and for everything that couldn't have happened without her, by the time my tears had started to drain, I remembered that Odile wouldn't have wanted me to just cry like this and overlook the many things she did represent, I recalled the way she'd hold her fan when she was trying to teach me to be graceful, this didn't really work out at first due to my innate wildness, when she saw that this wasn't working, she switched to teaching me the language of love, do you know how to signal *je meurs,* if you were to leave me?, and she was showing it straightaway, pointing the closed fan to her heart like a dagger, and she looked so tortured that one simply had to laugh, and how about my *bonheur* depends on your *unique* word?, showing this, too, by holding

the middle part of the open fan with two fingers
as her eyes radiated with devoted anticipation,
she just carried on teaching me such mischief
for all imaginable situations, she was an excellent
teacher and chaperone, exactly like I needed, and
there, under the chestnut trees, I was trying to forgive myself for having assumed that her zeal was
fuelled only by her passion for pedagogy, needless
to say, I didn't manage, it doesn't really work like
that, one can't just take a deep breath and forgive
oneself, only Brouillard and those of his ilk think
that, or rather make people believe such a thing,
they are the ones who wouldn't actually be in a
position to forgive anything to anyone if we didn't
live in this topsy turvy world, where the word of
God is being preached by people who have nothing to do either with this word or with God; I'm
now basically past everything, there is nothing or
no one for me to wait for, I missed the boat of love,
or I didn't miss it but it suddenly took to the skies,
akin to the orange of that magician I had seen in
Vienna shortly before my parents had announced
what I thought to be the most shameful decision
of my life, all the more shameful because it wasn't
actually mine but it turned into the most wonderful decision of my life, especially because by then I

had already been playing a role in it; rumour had it that the magician was capable of miracles, and his fame had finally made it to our castle following the many rumours, whispers, prattling and murmurs; one day, George, our English servant interrupted our lunch with a totally shocking lack of restraint considering his generally reserved nature, the high stewards nearly fainted from surprise, one of them had even spilled the sauce, *Tischbenheim, Tischbenheim*, our bewildered George kept panting rhythmically, his sweaty forehead just as disturbing a sight as his wide-open mouth, looking like a fish out of water, and it took a while until we managed to make him part with any information about this Tischbenheim, such as who he was and what he did, my parents had instantly fallen prey to this magician, like most unhappy people, they hoped with all their might that if obscure forces existed, then their disappointments weren't quite in vain, I, however, had felt a strong dislike towards this man right away, me of all people!, who was flying about in a completely random fashion that was impossible to follow even for myself, I was trying to fight this feeling but failed, while my new chaperone, the stern sister Helga kept nodding in agreement, and this alone was enough for me to hate myself; meanwhile George just carried on with Tischbenheim's achievements, he can boil an egg in his palm, grow an orange tree in an instant and such-like, until I dropped my fork and ran out of the dining room to the consternation of my parents, George and sister Helga, even if they didn't find my behaviour shocking for the exact same reasons.

It was impossible to send the magician away as my parents were entirely captivated by his talent, I couldn't grasp this, seeing that in general they looked down on servants from their aristocratic heights, yet they had literally fallen in love with the likes of George or Marfa, who were basically servants in terms of status, and what was even more eerie, they had completely lent themselves to the gossip and raving of servants, a hundred footmen and maids were racing from Vienna to our castle and to other nearby estates to enthuse about the unique abilities of Tischbenheim, as you can see, I wasn't prepared to forgive my parents anything, especially not around this moment in time, when frantic preparation was suddenly underway, with outfits having to be picked and packed and boots needing to be polished, the servants worked all day without as much as taking break, but this time I couldn't sense their usual sulk concealed under the guise of good manners, everybody was spinning like a spindle, and by the next morning, the four-horse carriage was ready to depart, the coachman looked more ceremonious and stately than ever before, and I only noticed that this was Hans when I took a closer look, even this, I mused, and then we set off, spending the next night at our chalet in Blauturm before triumphantly pulling in to Vienna; Tischbenheim had his own small theatre by the river Donau, everything was sparkling and glittering, large chandeliers were hanging from the ceiling and with the exception of the rows of seats and the stage, the place looked like any aristocratic castle, and yet, how different it was!, in spite of my foul mood, I couldn't refrain from letting myself fall under the spell of this environment, and that curtain, that mysterious purple curtain, which was just a prop like any other, and yet so unique and unpredictable like Tischbenheim himself when he finally appeared; this was carefully orchestrated, at first, a small hunchback introducing the man who was able to transcend the boundaries of time and space, these excessively elaborate phrases and wide gestures reminded me of Odile, when she was imitating ham acting, I was adamant to keep an eye on the faces of sister Helga and Pater Brouillard, who had joined us under the pretext that 'God will forgive me, just this once', we had nearly fainted by this point, but then Tischbenheim appeared and one could instantly see that these generally empty phrases were actually filled with life, a slim-faced, dark-haired young man stepped onstage, it was clear to see that he was both vulnerable and mysterious, and he also knew how to treat wounds, even if he wasn't able to heal them, soul and intelligence were intertwined in him in a most unsettling way, not to mention his added sensitivity, so when he asked after a few short and rather insignificant numbers which lady would like to help him, my normally inhibited mother almost fell out of her box in an attempt to comply, his request was for my mother to brandish her handkerchief and then let it drop, seeing my mother's hesitation, he gently magicked it out of her hand and thanked her with such elegance that she kept mention-ing this until the end of her life, following which he made the handkerchief disappear in a single move and started to talk about the weather, who wouldn't like to shorten a long and boring day and lengthen the brief moments of happiness, and who wouldn't want to experience happiness straightaway, he asked, lifting his index finger with a perfect sense of rhythm, by this point, the audience was gasping for air, so Tischbenheim peeled an orange, took out a seed and planted it into a pot he had prepared earlier, then sat down and focused while the audience just kept sighing, and within minutes, the magician had grown an orange tree and even threw two oranges to those sitting in the pit so people didn't think it was all fake, and concluded his act with the observation that happiness can arrive but also leave rather swiftly, within seconds, my mother's handkerchief reappeared held up by two butterflies and then vanished again into nothingness, my mother burst out sobbing, while I was fighting my disgust and fascination at the same time, all this was so theatrical and yet so true that I didn't even notice at first that the handkerchief was hovering in front of our box, my delighted mother grabbed it at once, thank you, milady, the magician expressed his gratitude with exquisite elegance, by which point even I found myself crying.

This was also the way in which my great love vanished, and sadly, it wasn't by way of butterflies.

Now that he has flown away so long ago, and dark birds are gliding past me and I'm not only hearing the beating of their wings but also feeling their touch, as they menacingly slap me every now and then, I really can't understand why we should live what's beautiful, unique and cathartic if we are to lose them anyway and these memories just sink into the bottomless ocean of time; of course, I can see how poor and helpless those who don't dare to lose anything are, perhaps happiness is none other than immersing yourself into the unknown and the hostile, you might even experience what's more familiar than the familiar in this way, I have lost everything and everybody, and soon enough, I shall also lose myself, and won't even remember what wouldn't have taken place without me.

Odile, Marfa, Anne and Tischbenheim— together with what happened to me with and through them—made it possible for me to grab Hans's groin, otherwise I would have been just like the two helpless daughters of my uncle Friedrich, who weren't endowed with either courage or imagination, mind you, these characteristics tend to go together most of the time, but who knows, perhaps, they actually were endowed with these but there was no one available to bring them to

the fore, seeing that they were surrounded with
the likes of George and Brouillard, Gertrude and
Luise would always behave in the most sensible
fashion and would be praised for their model
behaviour from our early childhood, those girls
from Budendunz!, my mother would piously
gasp, the girls from Budendunz!, my father would
growl in his reproachful voice, oh, there was no
way I could measure up with these girls, even if I
had ever aimed to achieve such a feat, Gertrude
and Luise were always impeccably behaved,
they'd always hold or produce their napkin, fan,
basket or handkerchief as they were supposed to,
they believed wholeheartedly in God, related to
the world in a moderately religious and intelli-
gent manner and were generally shocked at my
inappropriate behaviour, whenever we met one
another, we'd exchange greetings with well-man-
nered repulsion, I couldn't stand them, though I
had to admit that they lived a much less dangerous life than myself, but then again, who cares
about a life that is devoid of danger, I for one had
lost an awful lot, in fact everything at one point,
but at the same time, had won everything as well,
my cousins would probably fail to see this, despite
it being the truth, I was given the opportunity to

experience love, even if I lost it thereafter, what had once taken place cannot be altered at a later stage, he is no longer here with me and I can't touch his dear body, I had indeed made mistakes because I lived my life to the full, but why on earth should I bother with life if I didn't want to experience what living actually entailed?!

VIII

Truth be told, I'm living just like that at present, I had always thought that suicide was an escape route for the cowards, a while ago, however, I found myself rather envious of those who drown in rivers, such as the poor student fished out by my servants from the stream running at the bottom of our garden, I wouldn't have expected it to be so dangerous, or to end up envious of George, whose heart simply stopped when Marfa died, this had lent the ordinary man that he was a sort of spiritual nobility, by then, I was already in Syladia and only learned from my mother that a flock of red ravens had descended upon our castle that winter, they kept flying around the turrets, loitering in the park and around the chapel, sought refuge in the barn, and what's more, according to Mitza, the Romanian-born cook, one of them even turned up proudly in the kitchen and loudly demanded some *mămăliga*, that is polenta, the poor cook would always place a candle on the threshold thereafter, to ensure that she wouldn't be kidnapped by the devil, seeing that the red ravens had taken over the place, and when one of their colonels, perhaps the one that had demanded the polenta, issued a warning to Marfa with their wing, as if it were an index finger, she understood that she was about to die that very night, she said farewell to my parents, gave my mother that ominous red ruby, and withdraw with George to their abode, by morning, Marfa was indeed dead, and by noon, George too, they were given a joint funeral, love is cruel, Katerina, my mother rounded off her story and looked through me with sadness, I can't be sure whether this was because she hadn't experienced this cruelty herself, and it was only her instinct that gave her a clue as to what it might be like, or because I myself had the chance to experience this, or perhaps because my heart didn't stop despite having experienced this, so she was unsure whether I had actually been in love with the person I loved more than anyone.

For what it's worth, it may well be down to Odile, Anne, Marfa, Hans and Diego, and even Pasha Hayvan, that in these memoirs, this summary of my existence that is an unusual attempt to put some order in my life, I'm not coming across any linguistic hurdles, I'm simply writing a diary like that Transylvanian dowager, the daughter of a regional governor and widow of a count, who had come to see Prince Nicolaus in some landowner-ship-related matter, but my husband was unable to receive her so he asked me to handle this case as best as I could, I wasn't in a position to do anything for her, so turned to Chancellor Szipéthy in my fear, who was thrilled to attend to this task, even though he couldn't do it straightaway and I had to entertain the applicant in the meantime, when I went to look for her in the antechamber I found a frail woman with light brown curly hair framing her face, she must have had plenty to frame and conceal, I had never seen so much craving for openness in an introverted person, or perhaps not openness but understanding and acceptance, meanwhile, this face was also conveying the message that it wanted to be accepted on its own terms, begging for understanding yet stopping short of humiliating itself, it's preferable not to be understood at all than being understood on account of something other than one's true self, so I wasn't really surprised when after a short pause during which she kept scrutinising

my face, she asked whether I was writing a diary,
I immediately replied, yes, that's one way to gain
some freedom, to which she instantly retorted,
it's not possible to gain freedom, not in any way;
during the two short years I was there, I had often
thought of this woman despite never having seen
her again, on that occasion we chatted a bit longer
about where this or that snippet of memory might
belong, where exactly I should elaborate on this
or that episode, to which specific recollection it
belonged, I tend to have issues with such decisions and as soon as I finish writing, I cannot
stop thinking about how to continue the next
day, writing a memoir is significantly different
from writing a diary and I got seriously caught
up in the whirlwind of remembrance, it hadn't yet
slammed me against anything, perhaps this piece
of writing, these sentences and this feverish life, is
none other than a bang, because this is also a sort
of life despite not being life, not *proper* life only
a semblance, I keep deluding myself by trying to
relive what I had already lived once before, and
with this storytelling I now even understand
what had happened to me, storytelling has always
helped me understand everything, I never knew
what to make of experiences and theories apart

from drawing some conclusions, and I was never able to make any sense of the fact that everything was a station on the long albeit glorious road towards demonstration, I had never been able to separate facts from the context in which they had occurred, from say a smouldering gaze, a stupid face, a bow-back, an idiotic smile, anything that added a personal touch and made things harder to gauge; that said, I have never struggled with producing actual sentences, they seem to just rush under my quill, pouring out of my soul, and I find this a promising sign, even if it is a curtailed form of happiness.

This may well be some lame talent, I can't really tell, but I'm sure that what I was remembering seemed to be my time, mine and that of those whom I was mentioning and who had played a role in my life, and whose sole purposes seem to have been to assume this role, even I keep noticing with dismay that the vortex of writing didn't organise events in a chronological order but concentrated the mundane episodes of a quarter of a century in such a way that they appear equally valid at the same time, what I mean by mundane episodes is that they had happened to many others before me, many people had fallen in love and had lost the most beautiful moments of their lives, or these moments had become beautiful precisely by way of loss; on the other hand, these episodes were anything but mundane in the sense that they had happened *to me* and not to someone else, my mother, my father, George, Marfa, Anne, Hans, none of these figures would have come across the way I describe them if these events hadn't occurred to me, in that event this wouldn't be my life but the life of someone else who happened to grab a pen and started to mull over their life.

IX

So I grabbed Hans's groin, following which Hans came back to his senses despite his initial dismay, as I was to later notice with Diego, men do need this initial impulse, a moment of inspiration of sorts, so they can then show off their strength and be tough, even brutal with passion, but the first impulse has to come from the woman, I was crying out in pain when he grabbed my breasts with such ardour; pain belongs to the sphere of enjoyment up to a point, a point that, thank God, no one has transgressed so far with me, one craves pain not only fears it, or if one fears it, one also craves it, he stuck his tongue into my mouth and had I been more fragile, I would have felt it coming out at the back of my neck, I however was anything but frail or weak, so started playing with his tongue, nature is a wonderful principle, a wonderful spring, fountain, waterfall, I don't know what to call it, lava perhaps, in any case, in the right moment it grants people access to the kind of knowledge they need, in a way that they don't feel awkward about their earlier ignorance and about what they hadn't known before, as for me, the only previous relevant experience was deflo-ration, yet I lent him my tongue, my breasts bore the sweet pain, and later put Hans inside me as if I had years of experience behind me and had prac-ticed my skills for ages, as it happens, I was just an innocent girl, albeit a curious, perhaps even a reckless but nevertheless an innocent one, by the way, this makes me doubt the original inno-cence of any girl, I can't speak for men, but the moment our first period arrives and we begin our long and complicated relationship with blood, we can't be innocent, and I'd like to stress that being untouched, the lack of being exposed to men, is not the only hallmark of innocence, despite not having been touched by anyone until Hans, I was less innocent than if I had been touched by countless Hanses, because I was untouched by those whom I should have loved the most, or at least the ones I had the most to do with, and they didn't understand me because I was so dif-ferent from them, what else would innocence be if not a sort of willingness to understand, a sort of reverence to understanding, as if we were to say that I'd do anything just to spare you the effort, everyone whose gaze betrayed that they found something peculiar was someone who made no effort at understanding and who was also hard to understand, people don't really try hard, perhaps a little bit at first but then they give up, this cannot be understood, they say, and the person about whom they make these comments can't even be innocent after this, by the time Hans got to be moving to a rhythm in my lap, the others had long decided that I was weird, impossible to comprehend, strange, inexplicable, for them it was entirely irrelevant to whom I was to give myself and when, I had been long lost for them, to be fair, I wasn't really interested in their opinion either, for me, they were just a bunch of Brouillards, this name had turned into an umbrella term to denote an entire category, that of those deprived of imagination, whose solidarity against me could certainly try to break my reserve but not manage to actually change me.

Hans had pulled himself out of me at the best possible time, after that we just lay there next to each other and then fell asleep, by the time I woke up, Hans was no longer there, when I felt like flying, I took a joyful, contented and fulfilled flight, it was just like divine music, I had once heard someone play the organ and that experience was like this, I had never had any musical talent but like most girls of my age, I learned to play the harpsichord, Odile would always laugh whenever I was about to start, your hearing is fine, Katerina, however, your fingers are *agités*, and she'd pat me on the back of my neck with her fan, and we moved on to some other activity; I must have been around thirteen when our footmen, as with the case of Tischbenheim, brought us the news that a great musician would perform the next day in Leipzig, as it later turned out, he'd always play the organ there, but this time the footmen weren't as well informed as usual, Leipzig was only three hours away from us, so my parents decided that we should go, that week some particularly ugly styes had developed on both of my eyes, they was hurting and itching, I could barely see anything and had no desire whatsoever to listen to any musician but couldn't pull out of everything, so I went along because I had to, and although Leipzig was really close as I mentioned, we still managed to be late, I could sense people's disapproval despite being half blind, but the music was overpowering and I could feel as it carried me towards God, this musician by the name of Bach was playing the organ as if he were the very choir of angels, which invalidated my earlier conviction that talent had something to do with the demonic, because there was nothing demonic in this music, it was simply showing God-given talent and a sort of selfless- ness that I had hardly seen anywhere else; I didn't think it could have had anything to do with the exceptional, either, but this Bach had shown me the contrary, my two styes had vanished while we were still at the church, I could feel my eyes getting better and by the time we got home, there were only a couple of fading red spots to indicate that they used to be there, I was simply unable to forget this music, its rhythm has continued to orbit in me as it was orbiting that very night when I soared towards the sky, the moon itself was barely visi- ble but I had a moon of sorts shining within me, the splendid moon of my first love without pain and insecurity, it wouldn't have been possible to hope for anything more beautiful than this, and yet I was given the chance to experience it, albeit together with the kind of pain that is the prereq- uisite of any great love.

We carried on making love like this for months, with less and less caution, which wasn't really necessary anyway, the stars in Anne's eyes were sparkling mischievously, Marfa's Slavic colours got darker if she saw me, Odile looked at me with a sad smile, while the others failed to understand anything; every Sunday, Friedrich continued to beat Hans close to death, but now he cried even less, he was in fact more like laughing from within, and he was getting more adventurous in love, too, both of us were in fact, and thus got to discover each other's bodies, we were behaving like explorers from the very beginning, I bent down to lick his nipples and pushed my breasts into his mouth so he could suck them, I absolutely loved this, he was tender in a rough way, he couldn't help his stableboy hands, he couldn't chop them off or be born again but he was holding himself back, what could art possibly be other than restrained passion, even sculpted and wrought passion, with the exception of cases such as the conductor from Leipzig, all artists were striving to bring form to a formlessness that is in part the world, in part their own self and passion, and in order to show this, they can't do anything other than pluck this out of their self and with this movement already give it a form, this is a gesture that is both instinctive and considered at the same time, Odile had often said when trying to explain painting that it was a *passion travaillé, ma petite amie*, and when talking about Caravaggio, she had such sparks in her eyes that I could sense how close this iconoclast, and at the same time creator of form, had been to her, she liked this heavy-drinking brawler even more than Michelangelo and Tintoretto, although her way of presenting their art was unforgettable, too, she found everyone who had died young of unknown causes most relatable, and she was uncompromising in this matter; meanwhile, Hans had turned into an artist of lovemaking and so had I, it might have been on our fourth occasion of being together, when he was staring at my breasts so long and hard, with his eyes wide open and not letting me cover myself despite the cold, just stroking them, as if he wanted to incorporate their shape into his own being, but ultimately, his caresses made me feel his desire and in next to no time, we were at it once more.

The full moon carried on watching over us, and kept an eye on my extended flights because Hans had this habit of vanishing somewhere else and only appearing when I had long returned from the sky, and even if I asked something he didn't respond, just took me away, I got used to this ritual and was only wondering what would happen in the autumn when making love would be much harder in conditions of cold winds, even though it was fantastic to learn something new about the body I thought I loved, and because I hadn't loved anyone else before, I should be entitled to love indeed, and I shouldn't be ingrate and withdraw my love so easily, after all, this isn't a matter of choice of words, if I loved, I did love in earnest, but fate was on my side, on our side, and September turned out to be magnificent, with tart flavours and scorching heat, by then, he had kissed me a few times in the area where he entered me and I had also done that to him, but we refrained

from anything further, which was such a great
mystery!, I kept flying, hoping that I'd get rid of
my inhibitions, and on one of my flights I spotted
that wolf-man again, this time I could clearly see
that it looked like the creature about which Odile,
who else?!, had spoken to me, it was a giant being
whose wobbly walk reminded me far too much
of someone in order for me to be brave enough
to remember who it was, like last time, the creature stayed for ages at the meadow, sniffing our
food basket, howling at the moon at some length,
and then leaving at long last, Hans returned in a
little while, half-heartedly put our stuff away and
then jumped into the saddle without as much as
a word, and when I looked back from the horse-
back to the site of our lovemaking, in the middle of
Moon-milk meadow, I noticed a red raven, whose
inscrutable gaze simply stared back at me.

As soon as September came to an end, Octo-
ber ushered in a number of increasingly chilly
nights, back in the summer, Hans promised to
build a small cabin for us, however, nothing had
become of this plan, so our lovemaking turned
into a hurry-scurry and our art lost its passion,
retaining only its basic graft, meanwhile, Hans
started to restrain himself less and less and it felt

as if he was pushing me away even if he later asked for forgiveness, one time, when I didn't show my previous willingness to plant kisses on his whole body, he pushed me away with his full might, go away!, he shouted, got up and jumped on the back of Dusk and left me on my own, that was the last time I had taken flight from Moon-milk meadow, the red raven followed me in silence, holding its ground, and I just kept fluttering, even though I had realised in my heart of hearts that this was it, there must be a limit in everyone's life where love feels suddenly empty, it falls apart, deteriorates and crumbles, in my life, this love relationship had to come to an end at this very point, it couldn't be continued, My God, why couldn't I have had the wisdom I have now, when the great love of my life ended more or less the same way, perhaps because the lessons of one love affair cannot be applied to another, I was the same person, some-what changed in time, however, Diego couldn't have been more unlike Hans and my actual life couldn't have been more different from the life I had until then believed to be my real life.

Thereafter, during the full moon, I would often hear the wolf-man as he'd be growling and howling till daybreak.

These fast-paced and eventful years were
followed by slow and boring ones, I had no one
to turn to and I didn't even know that I could
turn to anyone, or to be precise, I decided that
I couldn't turn to my parents, and as if each and
every element had picked up on the inevitable
decline of my senses, I couldn't even fly anymore, no matter how much I wanted to, I was
badly in need of it yet it was in vain, I lived as if
immersed in a sack of salt, just blinking, breath-
ing and vegetating, unable to do anything else,
the red raven also stopped looking for me, Odile
died, Hans vanished as naturally as all inexplicable disappearances that everyone simply accepts
without asking for reasons that they might find
alarming, one night, Anne was knocking on my
window, but when I opened it full of hope, she
just looked at me, nodded with a sad face that
seemed to confirm what she had already known,
and swished away, no matter how desperately I
cried, she didn't turn around, and then I understood that everybody had given up on me; still,
I wanted to make another attempt and visited
the meadow where Odile had once wandered off,
back then, just as I was about to get seriously
concerned, she had charged out of the thickets

sitting on the back of a wild boar, this must have happened about two weeks before her death, a giant black-and-red hog charged out of the woods with Odile on its back, I immediately froze because all sorts of stories were circulating about wild boars, such as that they had once attacked one of my grandfather's grooms and ripped his mouth open with their tusks, after this the groom was known as the laughing man even though my father claimed that he had never seen anyone sadder than this laughing man humiliated by the boar, Odile, on the other hand, wasn't afraid, I could see this on her face, wild boar!, tusks!, she just kept slapping the back of this enormous beast, laughing, her French R's were terribly amusing, she carried on with this ride for quite some time, in and out of the thickets until she finally had enough, *arrêtez!*, she shouted at the boar, and it obediently stopped at once so Odile could jump off with her usual elegance, she waved with her fan and the beast clomped away, I ran up to her, hugged her and kissed her red cheeks radiating an otherworldly bliss, there you go, this must be the paragon of freedom, I said to myself naively as we started to make our way back home in the twilight.

I had also learned about the business of feeling bored from Odile, it's a truly aristocratic pastime, there's nothing better than being bored, seeing that it's mere pretence, come on, *ma chère*, let's be bored a little, she'd say every now and then, when she got fed up with teaching painting or geography or the art of prayer, that said, this day was unforgettable even by Odile's standards, or to be precise, by the standards I had applied to Odile, at times, we take pleasure in being able to measure our happiness, as if it could be measured, as if it wasn't happiness precisely because it couldn't, the day when she taught me how to pray we were sat facing each other for ages, I had to make the most devout face possible and this is difficult under all circumstances, let alone when someone is grinning at you and is watching your every move, pulling a devout face basically means being an *idiot, ma chère*, people tend to think of devoutness along the lines of casting an empty gaze like a forest devoid of birds, this analogy was typically Odile, I tried to imagine what a forest without birds would look like and my face must have conveyed something stupid because Odile burst out laughing, started to clap and to repeat that this will work, this will work, this made me pull an even more idiotic face because she quickly clasped her hands, as if she were to clutch this moment with her hands, too, and started to pray, Our Father who art in heaven, hallowed be thy name, she pronounced this word with so many L's that I had to laugh out loud again, miss, please, she said with unsmiling, even stern eyes that made me realize that she couldn't be joking, if possible, we should avoid jesting with God, and pulled such a sanctimonious face as if God himself was also present, sitting here and checking whether we actually respected him or only pretended to do so, thy kingdom come, thy will be done, these T's were so emphatic that they made me scared and fall under the spell of something sublimely inexplicable or inexplicably sublime, on earth as it is in heaven, by this point, that something was literally whizzing about in the room, so mysteriously and oppressively that I could feel why devoutness was such a serious matter, why Father Brouillard wasn't laughing at us and was rather abhorred of our laughter, I nearly started to respect this stupid man, Give us this day our daily bread, Odile said, having stopped sobbing, and forgive us our trespasses, I stopped laughing, not even from within, I didn't even want to, I only moved my lips, I didn't understand anything except for the fact that I couldn't understand anything, I didn't even have to understand anything, a fundamental inability to understand is actually required in order to have faith, as we forgive those who trespass against us, at this point, Odile started to squawk, screech and blubber, I have no words to describe what she did and can hardly imagine that she had either, in any case, it seemed as if the room had lifted up in the air and then vanished and we were suddenly kneeling in front of the crucifix in the chapel, Odile was crying and sobbing, not only shaken but literally rotated on a spit by sobbing, and she kept repeating, and forgive us our trespasses, as we forgive those who trespass against us. This was a horrible yet marvellous and uplifting day, and we didn't even get to the end of this one prayer only kept kneeling in front of the crucifix, all the same I ended up learning more about God, faith and religion than if I had been brought up in a monastery all along.

When we realised that we were cold and our knees started to hurt, Odile simply headed to the door without as much as looking at me, and by the time I got to follow her, all I could see was a blindingly white seagull circling around in the dark, always keeping to the same route around the chapel, and as I was standing there staring ahead, the seagull suddenly lost a feather which fell right into my palm after hovering in the velvety night for a while, but by the time I could have come to my senses, it burst into a blaze and turned into ash.

That night, Odile sneaked into my room. She must have kept watching me for hours, because she seemed very determined and stiff, with a straight back, yet also rather kind, and when I looked up, she started to talk, I couldn't interrupt her or ask anything, words were pouring out of her and a horrible story emerged in their wake, the story of a young girl, whose parents had been invited to a wedding in a faraway land; that was the first time I had heard about this awful place of which I heard so much later, the parents were members of the lower nobility so they considered this invitation an incredible honour, they went to the home of an Austrian margrave, accompanied by a great many chests and servants, the three of them travelled in the carriage for three weeks, and considering the length of the journey it was actually quite bearable, it was a splendid May, summer was about to burst out *and what an outburst that was*, Odile observed, she found it hard to learn certain words and others not so much, however, she had a rare flair for such subtleties, the three of them were desperate to get there, the girl was looking forward to the arrival itself, while the parents to the experience of this honour, suddenly there was a noise coming from the forest, some racket, rustle, shouting, commotion, followed by a gut-wrenching silence, and they understood that something irreversible must have happened; soon after this, a cheerfully wicked face knocked on the window of the carriage and greeted them in that barbaric language, he seemed to be smattering a little but most probably the message was that they were his prisoners, so they were desperate to find out what would actually happen; the foreigner ushered them out of the carriage with an impeccable politeness and then cut the throat of the girl's father in a single decisive move, she'll never forget that he had a heart-shaped birthmark on the back of his hand, the girl and her mother had no one to protect them after this, they embarked on a long and merciless journey, during which the man continued to be just as impeccably polite as before, without even touching them, still, he was utterly ruthless and chased them along tirelessly with his voice and omnipresence, his servants shook at

the mere sight of him and executed at once whatever he ordered them to do, one could see that
he wasn't just their superior but also a favourite,
consequently he probably wasn't the cruellest,
and indeed that was the case; two days later they
arrived at a bleak and eerie castle, where they were
led to an even eerier and more sinister countess,
the man may well have loved the woman, but
the countess most definitely adored him, to the
point of exaltation and self-destruction, they
couldn't object to the politeness displayed by the
countess even if it was cold as ice, like the tor-
ture chamber where they were taken; the girl had
to continuously wash the blood off her mother,
who couldn't have had any more openings into
which they didn't thrust various random objects,
as for the girl, they didn't harm her but she wasn't
allowed to turn her head or close her eyes because
in case she did, those swords, lances, knives and
pliers immediately delved deeper, the mother
screamed, begged, soiled herself but these two
villains weren't interested; on this occasion, Odile
was no longer crying, she sounded as if she was
telling a story, I gulped, unsure why she was telling this to me, every so often, they were given a
break to last longer, they were left to lie for days

on a bed of straw, eat the slop that was shoved in front of them and keep kicking the rats, but when they heard the footsteps of the man with the heart-shaped birthmarks, they knew at once that they were about to begin once more what they simply couldn't believe if it wasn't happening to them, screaming, agony, crying, begging, supplication, meanwhile God was nowhere to be seen, he must have had a very long sleep, the girl's mother died three weeks later, it's a miracle that she held out that long, towards the end she was nothing but a human wreck, as she lay dying, the icy countess suddenly caught alight, radiating, and charged at the man, jostling him to the ground right next to the girl's mother, the poor woman's last sighs mingled with the sounds of ecstasy because these two despicable creatures were moaning, shouting and murmuring raunchy words to one another while screeching through their teeth, at first, it was the woman's bottom that jived in front of their eyes, then the man's, and finally the girl was left all alone because her mother passed away and the other two got dressed, casting a contemptuous look at her, the girl was up all night, shaking with fear that she'd be next, she was sorry for her mother because she was deeply sorry for herself, but the next day, at dawn, the man appeared, Diego, this was the name the countess kept moaning into the straw, the blood, the excrement and the urine, while the man just repeated some strange name, with his impeccable manners, he washed the blood off the girl's face, covered her in rags and accompanied her to the edge of the forest, where he said good-bye in a most cheerful tone, from there, the girl did indeed head off somewhere and even arrived somewhere else but she still doesn't know where exactly she is, all she knows is that there is no God, or in case there is, then poor him.

Odile came to a halt at this point and stroked me gently, it wasn't even a caress in fact, she just placed her hand on my head as if she was giving me a blessing, this took us through the night till dawn, then morning and the next day.

XI

Often enough, there was no one to ease my boredom and then I had to revert to what I had learnt from Odile, when not even mocking Father Brouillard or everyone else was enough, I remembered that *la flaque d'eau toujours de l'aide*, so I started to look out for puddles, there were plenty of these at court, nothing was out of the question in this lousy place known as Syldania and yet such news simply filled me with disgust rather than joy, I wasn't sensing boundless possibilities only the limitation of boundlessness, so I kept staring at the puddles, needless to say, I had gotten to this level of bitterness after I had already met my divine Diego yet couldn't be by his side, so I was battling with the agony of jealousy, boredom and desire all at once, I cast hundreds, perhaps even thousands or millions of spells at the *flaque d'eau*, because it looked as if even nature was against me, yet Diego's outline simply refused to show, my lips were slowly cracking and I impatiently shooed everyone away who attempted to get closer, one time the chancellor went as far as to complain about me to the Prince in his roundabout way, but I didn't care, Nicolaus was incapable of telling me off in those days anyway, besides, I would have much rather stomped my feet and only my self-respect held me back from charging at the puddle, may it perish if it doesn't help!, Diego had just been dispatched to some faraway town by my poor husband, it wasn't his fault that I couldn't loved him nor that he had never found out what love was, as for me, however, why shouldn't I find out at least?!, it wasn't jealousy that made him send Diego away but the fact that he thought that in this muddy provincial world people were interested in dance, proper dance that is, not the one in which he-bears dance with she-bears; later on, Diego thought it would be amusing for me to hear that a few people did indeed turn up at first, out of fear for the Prince, but soon enough even this couldn't hold them back, so they brought brandy along and kept offering some to my charmingly heartless love, who naturally didn't accept it from these greasy-lipped punters and politely turned them down, until old Kanuthy made him so angry with his pig-like grunting that he took one look at the bottle and it shattered into a thousand pieces, and the old man got so scared despite his numerous campaigns against the Turks that he had to be led away from the scene by his son.

In the end, the puddle took mercy on me because an outline started to appear on its surface, at first, the sweet face, then the raven-brown gaze, the inexplicably yet undoubtedly merciless mouth, the jawline, followed by the shoulders, the body and suddenly the right hand, it seemed as if the puddle had all of a sudden produced this right hand holding something, I could barely make out what as it was barely visible, come on, show it to me, please!, at which point I had to gasp because the puddle did indeed listen to me and showed me what I asked, alas, it did indeed.

I was aiming to pay closer attention next time, but until then, I decided to stick with predictability, I was peerless in my patience and sobriety, people were literally flocking to audiences with me, because in only a few days rumours of the Prince's wife being a saint had spread far and wide, in a couple of weeks, even the initially incredulous had thrown in the towel and came to see me, our problems always tend to appear more powerful than our dignity, so I just listened to everyone, nodding, advising and giving orders, and continued to pray for Diego to give up his battle with this stupid crowd and tell Nicolaus that there was no hope, and indeed, he did give up one day, he informed the Prince who gracefully permitted him to return home, that first night of ours was just as unrivalled as all the others, and when I suddenly came to my senses, following our spells of lustful pleasure, I cast a glance at him and shivered with joy.

The past cannot be retrieved, it has since moved on, hope is futile, even if you revisit the location of earlier events, it is in vain, you'll end up disappointed, disenchanted and in despair, remembrance is the greatest magician on earth, it can pretend that what had vanished is still yours, and in a sense that's the case, except for the only aspect which truly matters and which could make you happy, I kept reminiscing about Odile and the boar, I will always remember them, yet it wasn't only Odile who was no longer there, neither was the freedom, the enthusiasm or the happiness I was in fact seeking, even the boar wasn't charging out of the woods, though I wouldn't have minded if it struck me down, mauled me or even took me on its back and darted off into nothingness, of course, it's easy for me to speak, had I really wanted to die, would I have cried out *Is this what you call happiness? Smelling the stench of an old man?*, why did it matter how I died if my life had to come to an end anyway, no, I had no intention of dying, but I wanted to make myself believe that this was what I intended, flying helped me see inside my own self and that of others, and I understood why so many letters and ambassadors were sent to my father, as if we lived at the royal court, to be fair, what could the ruler of a country whose princely garden is smaller than that of our castle possibly want, whose daughter could he marry, besides, I had influential relatives, by way of my uncles, I had the blood of various prince-electors flowing in my veins, so I wasn't a bad catch from a diplomatic point of view, my parents could see that I was melancholy, and perhaps Father Brouillard advised them not to give up studying the map until they find this Nicolaus, whom I then believed to be a token of unhappiness and who, in fact, later became the very guarantor of my true happiness.

The retinue arrived at long last, splendid horses, riders and carriages, my parents looked at me with joy and hope, thinking that this would

finally convince me of the validity of their decision, but I was already struggling with why it had
to be *their* decision, Arabian thoroughbreds with
gold-plated saddles and gold-plated headgear
above their starred foreheads, harp-playing swans
on the barouche, goodness, what a coat of arms, I
said to myself, feeling nauseous, everything was
far too nice to be true, and yet, this lie was the
truest thing in all of this, large swan singing in a
small garden, I might add bitterly and unfairly,
because that poor man only wanted his country
to flourish and to make it great thanks to my con-
nections, 'If God is with us, who can be against
Us? No one is, surely no one', he heaved a last sigh,
Count Ioannes even failed to understand why I
was so keen to see my husband's corpse, in his
memoirs he mentions this as if I had done something abominable, though all I was interested in
was to take a last look at the person with whom
I had lived a part of my life, and to whom I had
to give my body even though I would have much
rather chosen death, as it stands, death is not a
choice, or if it is, that's only for those who are
utterly pure and free.

XII

I arrived there after a journey lasting three days and three nights, Chancellor Szipéthy was in charge of bringing me to this faraway Prince, my parents let out a tear for me, as it was customary with brides heading to happiness, I did indeed head in that direction but I had no idea what to expect, I simply couldn't have any expectations, all I knew was that I was going somewhere, travelling, jolting in some carriage, it was September again, the leaves were falling and it was pouring with rain, I didn't give a damn about anything, I went where I was taken, if I had to get off, I did, if I had to sleep, I did, and only came to my senses when somewhere very far away from my home, but still not close enough to that old man, whose wife I was destined to be, I spotted a red raven on the chimney of a hunting lodge where we stopped for the night, at that point I figured that the world wasn't quite that grey, this tiny detail was comforting and energised me although I was

PÉTER DEMÉNY

dead tired, when we finally arrived and I got out
of the carriage on the arms of a knight, I was met
by a broken and long-suffering man with a long
beard, he was likeable enough though love is not
about empathy, neither in a romantic nor in an
affectionate sense, he told me what he had to say
and did this in earnest, his eyes gave it away, this
amount of suffering would definitely not sanction
lying, I stuck to my role, I had no other choice
and right after the speech I noticed a blade in the
crowd, it was hovering in the air without a grip,
followed by a pair of green eyes, at that moment I
knew that, despite all the suffering I had to endure
in order to arrive at this realisation, I didn't come
here in vain.

　　Looking back at my wedding, it was as glittering as the union between the prince of a faraway
country and the daughter of a margrave could
possibly be, I recall lots of hostile glances, being
anti-German is a tradition in that country, as I
later got to experience first-hand, everybody was
scrutinising me and I could literally feel the malev-
olently inquisitive gaze of the ladies and gentlemen
in attendance, only the ambassadors of the various countries looked indifferent, for the envoys
of the Bavarian Elector, the Emperor of Rome

or the Turkish Sultan I was an agent of power, I
could have easily had seven heads and they still
wouldn't have hated me, meanwhile the pastor at
court went on about the similarities between the
Virgin Mary and myself, I would have smirked had
I not been looking out for the blade, by this point
I had placed all my trust in that blade and the pair
of green eyes, they were roaming around somewhere, but I couldn't find them until the third day
when an exhausted Prince Nicolaus asked to see
me, I probably shouldn't even bother to mention
that tiredness was his habitual state, this time, a
tall and slender man was standing by his side, this
is the Spanish dance master, my elderly husband
informed me, Don Diego de Estrada, the man in
question introduced himself, his eyes were black
like the tuft of a titmouse and his mouth was
like a Toledo blade, and I forgot everything, the
repulsive wheezing of an old man as he was struggling to moan on top of me, this must have been a
change from his usual ways, the smell of his sweat
that was constantly lingering around, his embrace
that made me feel as if he'd been covering me in
mud, I forgot everything, absolutely everything
and all I could do was nod, he's at your disposal
for whatever you need, Prince Nicolaus continued,

and the man seemed to linger his eyes on me a touch longer than etiquette would demand, I nodded again and my Diego, who at this stage was just a beautiful man and a glimmer of hope in the night, nodded as well, the scorn that I later got to love and then hate so much was already visible in his eyes as he sensed my confusion, excuse me gentlemen, I said and took my leave, by that time a red raven was already scratching the window sill, we took a long flight, love, love, my wings swished, I craved love as I craved air, I had to love more intensely than I loved life in order to live, and when that afternoon I asked Diego to ride out with me the next day, the Toledo blade suddenly softened, mockery vanished from his eyes, ladies who are determined deserve respect, he said the next day, when I asked him about this transformation, why, the other ladies don't?, no, he replied, the others don't, and men don't either, life is not meant to be lived with uncertainty, 'seize the day?', I asked with a touch of sarcasm, to which he responded, oh, no, he wasn't saying this on account of Horace but of himself, there are many days we don't seize, and in any case, what would happen if we plucked every single day, only poets imagine such a thing, he simply thinks that in case an opportunity offers itself, he shouldn't miss it, what's more, and at this point his face turned pensive and started to beam so I shivered at the mere sight of it, at times he would even create such opportunities himself in order to then grab them, I hope I'm not tiring you milady?

No, his words had never been tiring because they made a lot of sense, and although I have no intention of denying the pleasures of the flesh and am happy to reminisce about them, because love is above all a bodily emotion and it doesn't exist without the latter, yet it wouldn't appear without some sort of spiritual connection between two people, either, this relationship emerged straight-away in our case, as soon as we looked into each other's eyes, this spiritual connection, however, didn't transform into a sensual one in the course of philosophical debates but by way of playful dialogue, after all, we weren't philosophers only two people who were pleased to find one another and immerse ourselves into this love as if it were a bath full of water, not having time for anything other than lengthy expeditions across each oth-er's bodies, time flies on its fluttering wings, it's essential to hurry up, even though back then we didn't have the slightest idea how much.

There was a light mist and this may have made me feel unwell, I read somewhere that it can cause shortness of breath, but it may also be that I had simply had my fill of the world, life, love and I couldn't contain any more happiness, how could I possibly deserve all this, what's certain is that I couldn't get any air and Swallow's every step made me more and more unwell, I don't know why I had to lie, oh, it's nothing, I just have no feeling in my feet, could we take a break here please?, needless to say, we stopped at once, he helped me off my horse, laid his riding robe on the grass and anxiously bent down to examine my foot, when I cast a glance at his hand I realised that I had never seen such hands, they were more feminine than the most feminine hand, really shapely and delicate, the nails were sparkling clean, the blue veins showed through his white skin and when he touched my foot that he had gently removed from my boots, I could feel that they were strong as steel, Hans was lacking the brutal sensuality of such tenderness and bluntness, this refined intuition, I panted as he gently twisted my foot, is it better now, milady?, he wanted to know, in response to which I urged him to just keep going if possible, and imagined him kissing my toes one by one and putting the odd one in his mouth, sucking them like chicken bone, unable to get enough of them, this made me feel light-headed, are you unwell, milady?, he asked and I replied in a harsh voice since he interrupted my daydreaming, I'm fine, thank you, I immediately regretted my sulk and as soon as I had my boots back on my feet, he put his riding robe on again and noticing my expectant look, he understood that I wanted him to help me get back in the saddle, Don Diego, make sure you hold on to what you have in your hands, I said, to which he replied, he can still feel what he had in his hands, and we rode back to the castle as if our lives depended on it, we were literally flying, and when Prince Nicolaus saw us he just nodded with sad satisfaction, this sad man understood everything, I remember, I kept thinking at the time that wisdom requires a touch of sadness and resignation, and a perspective grounded in the realisation that you are no longer a fully con-stituent part of this world.

My divine Diego arrived at court a couple of weeks before me, he was invited by the Prince on the recommendation of the Venetian ambassador as 'the most capable dance teacher in the world',

this was the unintended wedding present Nicolaus had given me, he had also given me another
one on purpose, a summer house he had built for
me in the nearby woods, I remember him telling
me one night when he was kept awake by pain
that he called it Sun Terrace because it was perfect
for lounging and soaking up the sun, you'll see,
Katinka, he told me, he did love me for sure and
this made him even more repulsive, how cruel of
life to make attraction so uncompromising, but
the summer house was indeed built on an ideal
spot on the mountain, with just enough space for
the wooden structure of the house and a small
garden, despite the cold it was warm, the sun was
shining above us and this in itself was warming
enough, for those in love, the sun was there even
if it didn't actually appear in the sky, when we
first went there with Diego, it wasn't just shining
but gleaming like the gold-plated bridle rosette
on Swallow's head, Diego's pert black stallion by
the name of Brisa was huffing and puffing as we
were trotting up the stony road, but every slope
comes to an end and after all my ladies-in-waiting
had left me, even my most loyal Lotte, a Bavarian
girl whom the Prince had put in my service out of
special kindness, Diego took me into his arms and

wasted no time in heading to bed, with his amazing hands, he peeled off my clothing and started
to caress me, his fingers lingered on my breasts,
then my belly, and returned to the breasts again,
he took my nipples between two fingers so they
perked up at once, I could feel I was getting wet
while he was stroking my belly again, discovering
my belly button with his middle finger, next, he
returned to my breasts though I could hardly wait
for him to head south, but he just kept fondling
my breasts, then kissing them, eventually sliding
his warm and softly-hard palm downwards until
it finally ended up where I was the hottest and the
wettest, he faltered for a little while, caressing and
cuddling me some more before he abruptly thrust
his finger into me, I cried out with pleasure, for-
tunately, the ladies-in-waiting had their rooms on
the other side of the house because I was unable
to control myself, in no time, his mouth was covering mine, but only for a second, just to give me
a taste, and already started to slip down my neck,
my breasts, my belly while he continued to thrust
with his finger, I had no idea that I could be this
deep, he then rushed back to kiss me, wildly and
rhythmically, passing his heavenly pace onto me
as he finally entered me, I was no longer able to

pay attention to anything by this point, all I could say were things I don't want to remember, or to be precise, all I want is to remember and to scream until screaming itself comes to an end.

I don't want to remember those words, despite wanting to remember everything in fact, and neither shame, nor any other consideration can hinder me in this remembrance, yet this doesn't really work outside that dual space which is in fact one, they would seem so idle if I wrote them down, so shameless, despite them not being even remotely shameful if we were back in the realm of love, it might be possible to return to the realm of love somehow, one could perhaps reassure oneself about having returned to the inner depth of love, however, one could never return to the place of pleasure except with the same person as before, however, this opportunity had left me for good, this was as obvious as it was initially clear that it would last forever, the scream came to an end and all I can remember is that I was flying, touching the sky, the Milky Way, the Moon and the Great Bear with my wings, and no matter how high I was flying, I could see Diego's face in the window, neither the half-light, nor the distance could hinder me in seeing him or in seeing him in his lifelike size, what is in fact life-size, a few minutes ago he appeared first as a giant then I couldn't even see him yet he was mine all the same, not *was*, he is still mine, how time flies, the afternoon aged into evening or rather rejuvenated into evening, the most magnificent evening in the whole wide world, dear parents, bless you, how could you come up with such a master plan, something like this cannot happen by chance, happiness isn't this random, although no one had planned or expected it, happiness is a blessing that must only be defined in hindsight, as I do now, when it isn't relevant anymore, he has left me and all I can do is console myself with his memory.

Until this was to happen though, I had plenty of opportunities to experience the caresses of these amazing hands, as well as his amazing body, every single vein of which I could feel inside me, whether I was on top or at the bottom, he always entered me as deep as to make my hopes cry out with joy, and every single nook and cranny of mine was crying, my breasts, my nipples, my bellybutton, my belly, my thighs, my bottom, and it came so natural to me to pleasure him as if I had always planned this and wanted this with this

man, and of course I always had, even if I myself
wasn't aware of it, love is what it is precisely
because it reminds people that they have never
wanted anything other than what they are experiencing in the moment, and that they have never
wanted it with anyone other than the person they
are experiencing it with at the time, in love, there
is no such thing as too much or too little because
love is exactly the right amount, anything less or
more would be a lie, so this isn't a matter of having
more or less, love simply is, for us, Sun Terrace
had become the ultimate high point of our lives,
a place of no return, at least for me, Lotte knew
everything, I could see this in her eyes, in these
metaphysical cows' eyes, I had never seen a gaze in
which stupidity and wisdom were so intertwined,
she was literally dribbling with dullness and yet
she understood everything, I would have never
gotten to the bottom of this secret if one night
a giant snow owl didn't pounce upon me, but
when I was nearly in its claws, it simply let me go,
majestically flying away, this experience repeated
itself with random regularity, at times, I even got
wounded since owls are dangerous birds, and
when I returned to Diego, our time together was
even more fabulous, we heightened what couldn't

be heightened any further while we could hear the sound of swishing outside, one such night, he told me the story of the Spanish grandee, who, to his misfortune, had acquired a new sword, I looked at him with indignant adoration, does my *pájaro* want me to stop killing, he asked, and I threw myself at him, shouting, kill me, kill whoever you want, darling, love is scorching and devastating and doesn't care about anything apart from itself, yet it's completely taken back if no one happens to bother about it either.

Love is a vortex, it cannot be anything else, in love there's no middle ground, everything is highly intense, I've never been interested in anything that wasn't intense, which is why I arrived at compassion so late, at a time when I'm basically no longer alive, I spat out and despised anyone who was lukewarm, even though they were also human, how could I have possibly known what hot meant, if there was neither cold nor lukewarm, it's additionally cruel of life that hot and cold meet each other at times, for instance in the case of Diego's actions and in Diego himself, who didn't even come to see me for days or perhaps didn't even think about me, after all he had to obey the Prince's orders and although Nicolaus really didn't care about us, he wanted to spare himself, and above all me, any gossip, Count Ioannes was always loitering around us, and in case he couldn't be present, seeing that he had never been invited to Sun Terrace, he carried out his intrigue at court by organising balls, one in each season, Diego couldn't be absent from these, the grand dames of Syladia were relying on his talent while their husbands were also keen to welcome him in their circle in their clumsy way, Regina Kovacsovszky, Anna Kende, Polixéna Báthory and Kata Palocsay were all lusting after my Diego, I saw what I saw, and to be honest, I was jealous, love doesn't like the idea of sharing and doesn't shy away from lowering the bar, one time, for example, I mixed some emetic in Diego's food so he was throwing up for two days, another time, I whispered to Brisa to trip over on the road, but then ended up praying that he wouldn't hurt himself, as it happens, this prayer was answered far too literally because Brisa passed away that same day, they couldn't even set off because the horse was already dead, the poor thing couldn't cope with the thought of harming its master or disobeying me, I was shivering with remorse and fever for days, and Diego understood everything and forgave me; one night, I was woken up by a strange noise and found myself twisting and turning without a clue, I was also a little afraid as it was only me and Lotte at Sun Terrace at the time, when I went to the window I saw a huge peacock flying across the night sky from the east, as if a colourful blade had been thrown into space, it looked at me in mid-flight and bowed its head, by the next morning, my fever was gone even if I wasn't quite back to normal, still, I slapped poor Lotte so violently for spilling some milk that she could only stare at me with joyful anxiety; the song of a peacock can only trigger unusual consequences, in fact, in love, everything has unusual consequences that isn't in close connection with the only thing that really matters: love itself.

XIII

At times, it was my duty to leave, because Nicolaus was either busy dealing with state matters while he could handle them, or was ill and hence unable to take anything on, on such days, I had to go to that dreaded castle, and although it was there that I had spoken to Pasha Hayvan and that female diarist, I hated the place, I was sick at the mere thought of it, love is a strange thing, as if it encompassed every single passion, this vortex is truly captivating and carries you away but it doesn't care about anything else, I didn't want to talk about anything else with Lotte, either, do peacocks sing? I asked her and she replied in a soft voice, I have never heard such a thing, milady, but this is because I didn't listen carefully, I didn't quite understand what she meant, but as I said, she was a rare mix of clever ignorance and stupid intelligence, and in any case, I had no time for Lotte, loyalty is overrated, we all talk about it but nobody really cares about it, having said that, Lotte is the only person I can still bear to have near me while I keep longing after Diego despite having no hope whatsoever to see him again in this life, still, these hellish days came to an end and Diego returned from the ball of Count Ioannes or someone else and our otherworldly experience took off again, this adventure of discovering each other's bodies, the questing journey of passion, the tingling, pampering, roaring and quieting down of my little shell, I dashed out of the window soaring to the sky, scattering my feathers in a shape that looked like Spain, I had studied Spain carefully on the map, this time, the peacock had also come with me and we sang the beautiful song of our love together, the love we simply couldn't or wouldn't want to get enough of, we didn't even believe that it was possible to ever get enough of it, one night, as we took a break from our embraces and kisses, I told Diego about my visit to that strange cave and about what that pair of eyes had told me, I quizzed him on the meaning of these words but he kept silent and that dawn we made love so arduously that I didn't even have to take flight in its wake.

We spent two fantastic summers together, because love knows a single season, the rest is a matter of habit and something that has to do with the calendar, the summer, with its heat, hysterical downpours and raging storms is best suited to describe love, it becomes one with it, for me, December was the hottest but then January turned even hotter and by February I felt like a cauldron, I thought that Diego felt the same way but blades heat up and cool down differently, I wonder whether he could have even been so hot if he hadn't been able to fluctuate, could I have loved him the way I did if he was more predictable, no, I don't think I could have but back then I was less understanding, Lotte had received plenty of slaps in the face for the most insignificant trifles but just put up with them and only fell silent when Diego had left me for good, at this point I had to feel ashamed again and am still ashamed because although I loved him enormously, I did manage to get over his departure.

This wasn't the only event that happened, there were many others and I shall talk about them now, honesty isn't only a matter of saying all sorts of bad things about ourself but also about other people, including the person we love, one time I was strolling in the Princely garden when my Diego was away, he told me that he was going

hunting so I was left to my own devices and had
to temper my rage, the rain was pouring down, so
my ladies-in-waiting tried to hold me back, barely
taking into account my rank, especially since
Nicolaus was on his deathbed, they would have
protested even longer had I not slashed the shape
of the cross into the air with my whip, I was wan-
dering among the raindrops and the alley of trees,
when I suddenly heard some noise from afar, I
scurried off in that direction but when I realised
whose voice it was, my steps slowed down of their
own accord, so he hasn't yet left!, I mused and
thought I knew it all, I sneaked a little closer and
as soon as I reached the edge of the trees I came
to a halt, I knew this meadow all too well, it was
the scene of my happiness, our happiness, what
did you tell her?, an older yet not exactly old man
asked him, we have never met yet he sounded
familiar without me knowing where from, in next
to no time, I guessed who it was, and the person
with whom I had lived all this and would have the
rest of my life, was repeating word by word everything he had whispered, murmured, shouted in
my ear or elsewhere on Sun Terrace, he showed
no sign of embarrassment and didn't seem to care
that this should have only concerned the two of

us, she's in our hands!, the older man cried out victoriously, in our hands!, he repeated cheerfully, and this made him even more familiar, he was already rejoicing about something only the two of them knew about, perhaps this hurt me the most, the fact that he had secrets with others, too, secrets that I thought could only tie him to me, hold on, father, a princess cannot be kidnapped so easily, Diego pointed out, but he couldn't even finish his sentence because a slap landed across his face, you've always been a coward, his father hissed, to my surprise, I immediately managed to take flight without any preparation, I haven't seen a single bird manage this, I buzzed and swished, nearly breaking the sky in two, I still don't know whether I flew up spurred by the insult to me or to him, what's certain is that there has never been a more beautiful and desperate bird in the sky, I kept racing and burrowing myself upwards, hoping that I'd never have to come down, but the sky is just as endless as hell is bottomless, and at that moment the sky was as hellish as it gets, I was flying among flashes of lightning but couldn't last as long as they; I never mentioned this unexpected and secret encounter to Diego, I suspect he might have known about it, I wasn't afraid of being kidnapped, it wasn't the worst thing that could have happened to me, for a while, everything just carried on as before, or rather not quite, something had cracked and even broken, something had come to an end and this couldn't be borne for long, and soon enough we split up, in a sense beyond emotional separation. That day, as on so many other days, we went for a ride in the woods, this was one of our favourite pastimes, but this time, we also went to make peace after our major quarrel the night before, I accused Diego of cheating on me with every single woman in Syladia, I was screaming and shouting, saliva spraying out of my mouth, I called him a womaniser and a debauched philanderer, his lips got thinner and thinner and when I dubbed him an evil Spaniard, he blazed up and slapped me so hard on the cheek that even my soul had started to sting, he stormed out of the room, I don't really know where he ended up sleeping but when I staggered outside in the middle of the night, I spotted the back of the peacock from afar, I couldn't even plead with him, he wouldn't have seen me anyway, but he did come back the next morning, people settle for so little, don't they, I was only hoping that nothing had happened, nothing irreversible had happened

in him, and as he was saddling his horse, I could
see on Estella's starred forehead that I was allowed
to tag along, so I had Swallow saddled and we
started off, it was summer, a waning August that
nevertheless kept picking up strength, the grass
was hot green, the air was fresh and there were
trees galore, our horses trotted in silence, so he
didn't get angry!, I thought naively, but he still
hadn't said a word, I was getting annoyed by his
sulking, I had indeed said some terrible things,
but even this was a testimony to his exceptional
status, wasn't it?!, so I was already bargaining with
myself, the path was getting narrower and all of
a sudden we found ourselves in front of a magnificent meadow, I thought this was a good sign,
the tree crowns had basically closed it off from
curious eyes and there was a spring to the right,
too, we looked at each other, he jumped off Estella
and then helped me get off, too, he spread out
his riding robe on the ground but then immediately vanished in the thickets, I got really angry,
he should attend to me, but then I just dismissed
this with a wave of my hand and lied on my back,
thinking that he'd find me anyway, I kept looking
at the sky and there wasn't as much as a single
cloud in sight, only the sun was blazing down,

it wasn't sultry-hot which I liked, being called a 'womanizer' isn't really an insult, I thought, and gloated about the slap, he must love me if he hit me that hard, something soft started to hum in me, as if I was listening to my own blood carrying my love, Odile swam by with her little basket, then Hans, Marfa, George, Anne, *all these distant memories*, someone in me must have thought, *people from the past*, the bang didn't bother me, it must be dry lighting, and I only lifted my head when I heard a noise, somehow the trees sounded rather strange, and as I looked to the spring I saw a giant wild boar soaring to the sky with my Diego on its back, everything was glittering around them, even the air went up in flames, I would have screamed but I couldn't let out a single sound, my Diego was hovering with his back to me and remained totally silent until he drifted away, until he floated away on the horizon, I knew then that I'd never see him again, I jumped up and started to fly, this was really hurtful, yet another boar!, no, one can't just get over this by way of a short flight, this needed more, much more, I flew all the way home and even then I wasn't done, I'm no longer flying though I would still like to carry on, if only my wings could break off like my heart was then broken, but nothing is being broken anymore, only an aging woman is poring over her notes and feeling ashamed that she had wrecked something she wouldn't have thought possible to ruin, she has been feeling ashamed for twenty odd years and still can't understand what happened to her, perhaps no one can, only I understand this pain, where it had come from and what it destroyed, or perhaps Lotte, who has since lost the faculty of speech.

XIV

Was it me who ruined it? No, not me. He did, because he couldn't control his urges, his temper, his desires. He ruined it because he showed me his other side, albeit inadvertently. But why was I so taken by surprise? Had I not sensed that just as great happiness has an unhappy side, ravishing beauty also conceals another facet, after all, who could possibly be interested in playing the flute of piety without the clang of demonic clarinets? Why can't I just be grateful that it *did happen*, rather than being obsessed with what did *not happen*? Who could guarantee that, in the absence of vileness, miracle would have still taken me in its arms? Where can one find a Diego who isn't *both* gorgeous and vile? Am I not expecting him to be an angel, without any bad qualities, yet also without desire and a heart?

The birds are about to peck at me with their beaks, ready to hurt me, I must make a concerted effort not to pay attention to them and fly out of the window so they can pick me to pieces. Stay with me so long as you can, don't vanish in the mist of my soul, dearest memory, my one and only hap…

HAPPINESS

HAPPINESS

HAPPINESS

MADNESS DIEGO

YOU SON OF A BITCH

PÉTER DEMÉNY (b. 1972) is a writer, poet, translator, columnist, professor of literature at Babeş-Bolyai University, and editor at the literary magazine *Látó* based in Târgu Mureş. He has published poetry, prose, essays, critical monographs, and literary columns. He has translated, from Romanian into Hungarian, several writers, among whom are Nichita Stănescu, Gabriel Liiceanu, Ştefan Bănulescu, Ioan Es. Pop, Ştefan Borbely, Alexandru Ivasiuc, Constantin Țoiu, and Eugen Uricariu. In Romanian, he regularly publishes essays, articles, and poetry in *Observatorul cultural, 22, Bucureştiul cultural, Ziarul de duminică, Apostrof, Teatrul azi, Corso*, and the online platforms *LiterNet.ro* and *Literomania*.